# WINNING HIS LOVE

## STARLIGHT RIDGE BOOK FIVE

### KAT BELLEMORE

KB PRESS

# ABOUT THIS BOOK

**He's done playing the dating game.**
**This small town won't let him quit.**

———

After spending six years in Thailand while working for a service organization and chasing after the only woman he's ever loved, Travis Matkin is done playing games. Desperate for a new start and a chance to settle down, he moves to California to manage a small-town hardware store. The people of Starlight Ridge are all too happy to have a new face and promptly set their sights on pairing Travis up with one of their many eligible bachelorettes —through a charity auction.

Eliza Meyer has always been competitive, and her beach volleyball team's five-year winning streak is proof. But she doesn't train hard to win—she trains hard to live. Determined to outwit the disease that has cursed her family for generations, she's doing everything she can to stay ahead of the game. Her competitive streak doesn't end at athletics, however, so when Starlight Ridge starts up their first community charity auction, she knows she needs to win. Eliza only wishes she would have realized what she was bidding on.

# ALSO BY KAT BELLEMORE

## BORROWING AMOR

Borrowing Amor

Borrowing Love

Borrowing a Fiancé

Borrowing a Billionaire

Borrowing Kisses

Borrowing Second Chances

## STARLIGHT RIDGE

Diving into Love

Resisting Love

Starlight Love

Building on Love

Winning his Love

Returning to Love

# 1

Travis adjusted his yellow and black plaid shirt in the hotel-room mirror. It was his favorite—his good luck charm. Over the past six years, it had faded. And as he'd sweat and worked under the Thai sun, he had thinned while his muscles had grown. He was an odd shape now, and the shirt didn't fit quite right anymore. Still, he couldn't bear to throw it away. And if anyone needed good luck right now, it was him.

All the same, he threw on a leather jacket over the shirt so it still showed and gave the illusion that it fit. He had a last impression he needed to make. Not that it mattered anymore. But still, he had some dignity left.

Travis grabbed the handle of his suitcase and took the elevator downstairs to check out. The Thai receptionist placed her hands together in the traditional *wai* gesture and bowed. He returned it. Would that be the last time he ever bowed his head to someone, a sign of greeting and respect? He blinked moisture away, handed his room key to the receptionist, and walked outside into the heat.

Chloe and Davis were waiting for him, leaning against a dented Jeep parked against the curb. Chloe looked good, her hair pulled up into a ponytail, sunglasses perched on her head. Travis couldn't help wondering for the hundredth time what Davis had that Travis didn't. Davis certainly looked more like he belonged in the country now than when he'd arrived several weeks ago. And the man was an expert craftsman. He knew his stuff and could singlehandedly build a Thai hut better than even Travis. Not that Travis would ever admit it.

But still.

Travis had always thought it would be him and Chloe. Of course, he'd also thought he and Janet would be together forever.

The Jeep.

Dry mud caked her sides. That Jeep was like an old friend to Travis. He'd always been the one to drive her through the jungle, picking up volunteers from the airport, going into town for food and supplies—no one drove her except for Travis.

Who was going to drive her now?

Surely not Davis. The Jeep wouldn't last a week with him at the wheel. Travis wished he could take it with him. Protect it.

"You really didn't need to take the time to drive me to the airport," he told Chloe and Davis as he walked the short distance to where they waited. His legs felt heavy. Like they didn't want to go any more than he did. "The hotel has a shuttle."

Chloe snorted. "Since when have we ever allowed someone from Building for Hope take the airport shuttle?"

"It's not like I'm a starry-eyed volunteer," Travis said, lifting a shoulder.

"No, you aren't. You are much more." Chloe stepped forward and, placing a hand on his arm, stopped him mid-step. She lowered her voice. "I'm sorry things didn't work out how you were expecting, but I want you to know that I still consider you my closest friend. And maybe it was selfish of me, but I needed this goodbye. I needed the final farewell. And I'm serious when I say that I hope you come back to visit."

Travis's breath caught in his throat. He supposed he'd needed a final goodbye as well. Closure. Maybe Travis could return to Thailand someday, but not as long as Chloe's presence made his heart beat so hard that it ricocheted off his ribs and made him sick at the thought that she didn't return his feelings.

His gaze dropped to where her hand still rested on his arm. "Thanks. And who knows? Maybe I'll come back. One day. Or maybe I'll love Starlight Ridge so much, I'll never want to leave." He gave her a lopsided grin.

One that Chloe wouldn't believe for a second. She knew him too well for that.

She gave a sad nod and retracted her hand.

Travis knew he wasn't returning to Thailand. And he doubted he'd ever love a place as much as this one. This had been his home for the past six years, and he'd hoped forever.

At first Travis hadn't known where he was going to go, he'd just known he needed to leave. He had thought about back-packing through Europe, doing odd jobs to earn money along the way. And then an opportunity had presented itself. One that Travis still couldn't believe he'd agreed to.

Travis would take over Davis's hardware store in his little Californian hometown, since Davis had managed to do the impossible—swooped in with his good looks, overly sensitive personality, and poor taste in clothes, and stolen Chloe's heart.

Travis couldn't stay and watch another man living his life— the one he'd felt he was meant to have. And so, Travis was taking over Davis's life. Taking over for the man who had taken his place.

Ironic was what it was.

And tragic.

Davis reached for Travis's suitcase to place it in the back of the Jeep, just as Travis had done for Davis at the airport all those long weeks ago.

It wrenched Travis's heart just a little tighter. If only he'd known then what he knew now.

"This all you got?" Davis asked.

"It's all I've ever needed."

Well, not quite. But he supposed you couldn't have everything, could you?

## 2

Alone.

It wasn't a feeling Travis was used to.

His gaze swept over a picturesque boardwalk, taking in the many stores surrounding the one he was meant to manage. A chocolate confectionery. Scuba shop. Dry cleaners. An Italian bistro that announced its grand opening. There, in the middle of them all, was a large sign that simply said Hardware Store. The sign was neat, taken care of. That was more than he could say for the store itself. Dust and dirt clung to the windows, the CLOSED sign a cheap thing that hung on the other side of the front door.

In spite of the warm day, no one else was out walking the boardwalk, though Tavis could see quite a few out on the beach. He was tempted to join them, but he had a job to do and turned instead to his store.

Not his, exactly, he thought, as a weight settled in his stomach. He didn't own it. Didn't even pay rent. Travis had been hired to manage it and in return would earn a paycheck and use the apartment above the store. All he needed was to make sure that the small town of Starlight Ridge could purchase the tools and supplies they needed or, hopefully more often than not, go out and be the one doing the repairing.

Travis wondered if he'd even have business, judging by the lack of people walking about.

He rubbed an eyebrow. This was a mistake. Coming here. Thinking that this place could help him get over Chloe. Thinking it would help him start over.

Rather than the constant movement that Travis was used to —that he needed—this small town felt like time had stopped, everything on pause. The opposite of what he wanted. Travis needed something that would keep him busy, occupy his thoughts. He needed something to do.

In Thailand, Travis had been in charge of a dozen hormonal college students who had wanted to pad their resumes with things like "helped build huts in the middle of a Thai jungle," all while hoping to do the least amount of work required. What they'd really wanted was to have plenty of time to explore the country, go on elephant rides—experience adventure. And of course, squeeze in a romantic fling or two. Sure, they wanted to help people. But they wanted to have fun while doing it.

Work wasn't always meant to be fun.

And romance couldn't be counted on.

Ever.

Travis would know.

It was what had driven him from Thailand after six years of heat and humidity.

And he missed it. Desperately.

He hadn't realized how much he'd miss the giant tent he'd had to share with a dozen other people. The sounds of hammers and saws mixed with the caws of exotic birds. The monsoon rains that forced you to run for any available shelter, or the alternative—getting caught in one and not bothering to hide because after two seconds you were already soaked.

Travis released a deep sigh and walked up to the hardware store. He tried to see inside through the front window, but it was too dirty. He squinted, as if that would increase the visibility of what lay in wait for him. It didn't.

Davis had given Travis a key to the store as he and Chloe had driven him to the airport. He'd made Travis swear that he'd take good care of the key. Apparently it was the only one, and no one could make another for Travis if he lost it, because Davis had also been the locksmith.

That was the first thing on Travis's list of things to do today. Make more keys.

Travis slipped the key into the lock on the front door, and it turned easily. Pulling in one last long breath, he stepped inside and worked to find a light switch. Florescent lights flickered on, illuminating the neatly kept shelves, everything in its place.

Regret.

Despair.

The emotions hit hard.

This was his life now.

Instead of working outside all day, he would be stuck in this place. A place full of tools that he wasn't meant to use.

Travis hoped that Davis hadn't been exaggerating when he had said that he'd spent most of his time fixing things around town rather than behind the checkout counter. Travis didn't think he'd be able to handle being inside this place longer than an hour at a time.

His pulse quickened.

What had he done to end up in a place like this? Where had he gone wrong?

His breaths shallow, Travis quickly backed out the way he'd come and moved outside, closing the door behind him.

He stepped away from the store and forced himself to breathe. His heart began to settle. Out here, he could almost convince himself that he was on break visiting Pukket, or another Thai beach.

Almost.

The air was different here. Quiet. It didn't have the thrum of chaos that seemed to permeate Thailand. Even when he'd been living in the middle of nowhere, there had been life everywhere he'd looked.

Here? There were the waves. And the birds scavenging along the sand, hoping to find remnants of food left behind by beach-goers. Davis had asked Travis if he was up to it—handling a small tourist town.

Anything Davis could handle, Travis could. So of course he'd said he was up to it.

Travis was suddenly unsure that was true.

Of course, anything was better than the alternative. Staying in a place where the woman he loved didn't want him—saw him as a friend. A reliable worker.

Turned out that, even as a builder, he was replaceable. By Davis of all people. Except, Davis had gotten the better end of the deal. He'd gotten both the job and the girl.

Travis's gaze traveled to the ocean. Even though he really needed to get the store cleaned up, the dusty shelves and dirty windows could wait an hour.

Right now, he needed to be anywhere other than here.

So, he walked the boardwalk, his hands shoved in his pockets. When he ran out of boardwalk, Travis took a left and moved toward the beach. He was surprised at how fine the sand was. So fine that after several steps, the small grains had already filled his shoes. He slipped the shoes off, then stuffed his socks into one of them before continuing his walk toward the waves.

A group of bikini-clad women were playing beach volleyball, and he quickly steered clear of them. Several years ago, his reaction would have been quite the opposite. He would have flirted, asked if he could join in. But times had changed, and so had he.

Travis spotted a lifeguard station and walked toward it. A man was sitting in it, shirtless. He was toned and tanned, despite it being late April. And he was reading a book. Didn't even notice when Travis walked up.

"Hey," Travis called up. "Is it always this quiet around here?"

The man started and sat up, his book dropping to his lap. He immediately scanned the ocean, looking for threats. When he realized there were none to be found, his gaze landed on Travis. It took another moment before he seemed to remember the question and he finally answered. "No, not during tourist season." He settled back into his chair. "You came at a good time. Spring breakers have pretty much dried up, but summer tourists will start flooding the beach in about three weeks. How long are you staying?"

That was a good question. Unfortunately for Travis, he was stuck here for the time being. If he'd had a plan B, he would have already been back on a plane.

"Don't know," he said. "A while. I'm managing the hardware store up on the boardwalk."

"The hardware store?" That made the lifeguard sit up straight again. It seemed they didn't have a lot of turnover in this kind of place.

"The owner is supposed to be flying out tomorrow to get me situated and teach me the ropes."

"The owner," the lifeguard said slowly, like Travis couldn't mean what the lifeguard thought he meant.

Travis gave a hesitant nod. "Yeah. His name is Davis. You know him?"

"Everyone knows everyone around here." And then the lifeguard jumped down from his station and stuck out a hand. "I'm Isaac."

Travis wasn't used to handshaking—it wasn't a thing in Thailand—but after a brief hesitation, he took the outstretched hand. "Travis."

"Is this a...temporary situation?" Isaac asked, leaning against the lifeguard station. When Travis didn't answer right away—unsure what the lifeguard had meant by the question—Isaac tried again. "You planning on staying long-term?"

Travis turned his gaze to take in the ocean and the town's colorful shops. "Maybe. Might be a good fit."

That seemed like a diplomatic enough answer, and it wasn't technically a lie. He wanted to like it here. It was quiet, and beautiful. But Travis had just arrived and already had itchy feet —the need to run. And keep running. This was just a pit stop along the marathon. A chance to catch his breath before continuing. Only problem was, he didn't know where the finish line was.

Issac nodded slowly, like he still wasn't sure what to make of Travis's presence. "Strange that Davis hadn't mentioned anything about leaving town. You know where he's moving to?"

"Thailand."

Isaac tilted his head, pantomiming pouring sand out of his ear. Like he couldn't have heard right. "Uh...we're talking about the same Davis, right? Davis Jones?"

Travis's lips tilted up into a smile. He knew exactly what the lifeguard meant—and he'd had the same thought when he'd first met the man: How would he ever survive? "You wouldn't recognize him over there. Thailand brought out a different version of him. The real one, I think. I'm sure meeting Chloe didn't hurt either."

"So, he met someone." Isaac's face lit up with a boyish grin. "Good for him."

Travis tried to ignore how much that statement pained him. Made him feel things he'd been trying not to feel.

But that was nothing compared to what he felt next—an object smacking Travis in the head so hard, it felt like his teeth were rattling. He grabbed the railing of the lifeguard tower and waited for the stars to clear.

Out of the corner of his eye, he saw a woman running after a ball as it rolled toward the ocean. Her long hair was piled into a messy bun on top of her head, her skin red from what looked like landing in the rough sand several times too many.

"Sorry," she called over her shoulder. "It doesn't normally get away from me like that. If that's how we play in the tournament, we won't make it past the first round." She scooped up the volleyball and turned toward where her team waited, but Isaac called her back.

"Eliza," he said. "This is Travis. He's going to be managing Davis's place for a while."

Eliza turned back toward them, an eyebrow cocked. "Is that so?" She threw a glance at Isaac. "Does Jessie know?"

"She probably knew before Travis even arrived."

"Who is Jessie?" Travis asked, his words slow. The way they were talking, it almost seemed like she was the gatekeeper of Starlight Ridge—the bouncer. The one no one got past without permission.

Eliza was quiet for a moment, like she was trying to figure out the best way to say it. "Everything that goes on around here is because of Jessie. But more importantly for you, she's head of the welcoming committee. So expect to not have to shop for the next week, because with all the food baskets you'll be receiving, you won't go hungry." Eliza glanced back toward her teammates, who were calling for her to hurry up. "Gotta go, but nice meeting you." And then she disappeared, but not without another confused glance over her shoulder.

So, he had been right about Jessie. She was the bouncer. Welcome baskets were her way of being first on the scene and warning the town, if applicable. He'd grown up in a small town. There hadn't been welcome baskets, but they had had a Jessie of their own. An eighty-three-year-old woman named Edna. And Travis had feared all ninety-two pounds of her.

"You dating anyone?" Isaac asked, his gaze flitting between Eliza and Travis. "Got someone special back home?"

That seemed a bit of a personal question, considering they'd known each other all of three minutes.

Another pang in Travis's chest.

Isaac watched him, waiting for the answer. He was in no hurry and looked like he didn't mind waiting all day.

Travis shoved his hands into his pockets. "No. Life in Thailand wasn't very conducive to that kind of thing." He hoped that Isaac wasn't getting any ideas. Travis wasn't interested in dating, and, no offense, but he definitely wasn't interested in someone like Eliza. He was done with the beach volleyball type. Travis had had plenty of those opportunities in Thailand, and he wasn't going to waste his chance to start over.

It was time for Travis to show the world that he was more than just a set of muscles—not just the guy who could do all the heavy lifting.

Except, he didn't know how to prove that yet. Or why he wanted to.

## 3

Eliza placed her hands on her hips and surveyed the group of women gathering up their belongings. She'd pushed them hard for the past two hours—she hoped not too hard. These were the women she spent every morning running drills with. Her friends. Her teammates. And they were good. And dedicated. But would it be enough to grab top spot in the beach volleyball tournament this year? Teams traveled from up and down the California coast to compete in the month-long tournament, and the other teams had always been just that little bit better.

Last year Starlight Ridge had come in fourth, which wasn't bad out of fifteen teams. But Eliza wanted that trophy. The one that said they were the best—that they had worked the hardest.

"What do you think of running two-a-days until the competition?" she asked as her team hoisted their bags over their shoulders. The expressions on their faces said it all. They didn't want another practice—what they wanted was a shower. And probably a nap. Anything that wasn't volleyball.

They shared looks that said they were trying to figure out who would be the bearer of the bad news.

After a few seconds of awkward silence, Bree stepped forward. "I know we didn't do amazingly well today, but we really are doing the best we can." She paused. "Most of us joined because it sounded like fun. My toddler keeps me occupied all day, and being part of a team sounded like just what I needed. But pushing us through more drills and moving to two-a-day practices? That's not something I'm interested in."

The other women gave little nods of agreement.

A storm of annoyance brewed in Eliza's chest, and she worked to shove it down. So what, she was the only one who truly cared about the competition and the other women were just trying to escape the mundanity of their lives. Hadn't that been how Eliza had gotten them to join the team in the first place? She'd told them that they'd get together each morning, hit the ball around, get some exercise, and have the opportunity to travel and meet players from other towns.

Eliza supposed she'd expected the fire of competition to catch once they were in practice. And she couldn't deny that they worked hard. But the truth of the matter was that, if anything, they disliked the competitive aspect more than when they'd first joined two years earlier.

Fine. They didn't care about winning. No problem. Eliza would carry the team to victory. They'd thank her later. And they'd realize how great being the top contender was. By the end of the summer, they'd be begging her for two-a-days.

Hey, it could happen.

She plastered on a smile. "We'll keep it to just mornings, then, no problem. I'll see you guys tomorrow."

Eliza gave them a small wave and slipped on her tennis shoes. And ran.

A few men whistled at her as she tore down the beach. She glanced down, just now seeing that she'd forgotten to put on her coverup and wore nothing but a bikini and exercise shorts. She ignored them and kept going.

Eliza ran to forget. To pretend. She did it so often, she could go several miles without even realizing it. Her feet hit the packed sand, still wet near the edge. Eliza veered so that she ran right alongside the ocean. Water sprayed each time her feet pounded down, but she relished the cold bite of the water.

It was probably thirty minutes before Eliza remembered she was supposed to cover for Isaac on lifeguard duty right after practice.

Crap.

His wife, Leanne, needed him up at the bed and breakfast that they owned, and Isaac had made Eliza promise she'd hurry over to the lifeguard station as soon as the team was finished, or it would be Eliza who would be explaining to Leanne why he was late.

Eliza loved Leanne. But the woman was also a Hollywood screenwriter and a business owner. And she took both very seriously. Eliza didn't want to be the one to make Leanne late for her online business meeting with Hollywood executives. It would not end well.

Eliza did a one-eighty and practically sprinted the entire way back, not stopping until she reached the lifeguard station. Isaac was standing next to it, sunglasses on, arms folded, as if he'd been in that position the entire time she'd been gone, just waiting for her return.

"I know, I'm sorry," she said, bending over and resting her hands on her knees. It was rare that she was this winded, and her breaths came quick.

Isaac had a nervous energy about him that told her he really needed to get going, but when she glanced up, he was watching her with his lips pulled up into a smirk. "Can I leave, or are you going to pass out the moment I'm gone?"

She straightened. "I'm fine."

"Good. Once you've caught your breath, call Leanne. It needs to be before I arrive, because you are not going to be the reason I'm in trouble. Not today."

Eliza folded her arms over her chest, as if that would make it any less noticeable how hard she was breathing. "Of course. Anything for you, Isaac."

"Glad to hear it. Because I also offered your services to Travis. You know, the guy you nailed in the head with your volleyball earlier. Figured it was the least I could do."

Eliza's heart stalled and her breathing with it. "You do know that makes it sound like you're hiring me out as something completely inappropriate, right?"

Isaac just grinned and took a few steps backward as he gave her a quick salute. "Meet him at the hardware store right after your shift. Don't worry, he said he can pay, and I know you could use the money."

"That makes it sound even more scandalous," Eliza called after him.

"I know."

And then Isaac turned and ran in the direction of the board-walk, but not before calling over his shoulder, "Remember to call Leanne."

AFTER SEVERAL HOURS of staring out over the ocean, only a few people braving the cold water today, Eliza took off her whistle and jumped down from her seat. Further down the beach, she could see her replacement, Luke, making his way toward her.

Eliza's stomach growled and she realized she hadn't eaten anything since before volleyball practice that morning. She would grab lunch from the diner, then work her way over to the hardware store. Isaac had no doubt hired her out for some kind of manual labor, and she could use the protein.

When things got crazy at the bed and breakfast, Eliza often helped clean rooms, which was why, she supposed, she was the first person Isaac had thought of to help the newcomer.

When she arrived at the hardware store an hour later, the front door sign was flipped to CLOSED, but Eliza doubted anyone needed the sign to tell them to keep away. Dirt now caked the windows, thanks to a couple of good thunderstorms the previous week, and it was obvious no one was currently manning the place.

Folks had known Davis would be gone for a couple of weeks, and it hadn't been a big deal. Live with a squeaky door or wait to buy those nails—you could do that for two weeks, no problem.

But then Davis hadn't returned, and people had started wondering. Sure, they could live without their handyman for a little while, but could they for a month? Two months? They had started worrying that they'd need to start fixing things themselves and buying supplies in the big city, or worse, try their hand at online shopping—something that most in town refused to do. Not only were they adamant about not wanting to support those large corporations, but the rare time that someone had actually ordered something online, it had gotten lost in the postal system and never arrived.

Eliza assumed it had been a fluke—it wasn't like they didn't receive letters and postcards. They did have a post office, albeit a small one. It was set up in the local jail, mostly because their postman, Charlie, said he needed the extra space to sort the mail. So now he shared the area with the local sheriff, Art, and they spent most of their time playing cards. Even if the townsfolk got their letters a day or two late, they eventually got them, or could stop by and collect their mail themselves, and that was just fine by them. No need for that fancy two-day shipping from halfway across the world.

Eliza peeked in one of the dirty windows but didn't see any movement, so she tried the doorknob. It turned easily, and the door opened. Everything looked just as Davis had left it, aside from the dust, and she expected him to walk in from the back room at any moment, his expression indecipherable and all business.

Except, it wasn't Davis who walked in from the back. The new guy—Travis—stepped out, shirtless, oblivious to Eliza's presence as he used his crumpled T-shirt to wipe sweat from his brow and then tossed it in a corner.

Eliza froze, unsure what to do, wanting nothing more than to escape his attention. Maybe she should sneak back outside, wait five minutes, then loudly announce her arrival. Give him a chance to put his shirt back on.

Had Travis had those muscles earlier? Eliza couldn't recall, her mind had been so focused on the game. His high level of attractiveness might have registered, vaguely, but it hadn't been enough to keep her attention.

There were more important things in life than hot guys. Or so Eliza had thought. At the moment, she was having doubts.

It took a minute, but Travis eventually turned his attention to a shelf of power tools along the back wall of the store, and Eliza seized her opportunity.

Dropping to the floor, she crawled behind a shelf containing packages of nails, screws, and other assorted fasteners. Once she reached the end of the aisle, all she had to do was take a left and she'd be home free.

Except, when she reached the end of the aisle, what she found was a pair of work boots. Legs were attached to those boots, and as Eliza's gaze shifted upward, the new guy's insanely

amazing abs took focus. She scrambled to her feet and was met
by a raised eyebrow and laughing eyes.

"Lost something," she blurted out. "An earring."

Travis gave a pointed look at her bare ears. They weren't
even pierced. And why would she still be in exercise clothes and
wearing earrings, anyway? At least she'd managed to slip on a
shirt over her bikini—unlike someone else. The difference was
that Travis didn't even seem embarrassed that he was walking
around showing off his muscles to anyone who would look.

She couldn't stand guys like that. Attention seekers were
what they were.

Eliza straightened and looked him directly in the eyes. "I
mean, my contact." *That's right, keep it cool.* "From my right eye.
All the dust in here made my eyes get all watery, and POP, there
it went. Right onto your dirty floor."

Eliza could tell she was losing him. The guy was looking
more amused than anything. She needed to reel it in, not let her
overactive brain get away from her. "I won't bother looking for it,
because I'd probably get pinkeye if I tried putting it back in. Or
an infection of some kind. Whatever you can get from dirty
contacts. Anyway, I should probably get going now that I can
only see properly out of one eye."

Travis stepped back and motioned with one arm toward the
front door, not bothering asking questions or trying to stop her.
Just kept looking at her with that annoyingly handsome face of
his. His lips seemed to be upturned into a perpetual half-smile,
and it was driving Eliza crazy. Just staring, smiling, not saying
anything.

Eliza took a step toward the front door but then stopped and
swung back toward him. "Isaac sent me. Said you needed my
skills."

Travis's smile didn't fade, and if anything, it only grew. He folded his arms across his huge bare chest. "Is that so?" Eureka, the man could speak.

"Yes." Eliza tried to stare at a spot just beyond Travis's shoulder. "Said you would be paying me to help out."

He gave a small nod. "You're the volleyball player."

"Uh-huh." Her voice came out as little more than a squeak.

"You going to be okay working with only one contact?"

Eliza tilted her head. "Contact?" She didn't wear contacts. Oh, right. Yes, she did. Because she'd just lost one. "I mean... yeah, I should be okay."

Travis watched her for a moment longer than was comfortable, then turned and strode toward the back of the store. "You're earlier than I expected, but that's good. We have a lot of work ahead of us."

Was she expected to follow him? She wasn't sure, but he wasn't slowing down or checking to see if she was keeping pace, so she hurried after him. Right as she had managed to close the gap, he stopped at a door to his right and swung it open.

Eliza put on her internal brakes and managed to stop just before hitting the door, but the effort threw her off balance and she fell back onto her butt.

Travis closed the door and held up a bottle of window spray and two rags. When he saw her on the floor—again—he merely smiled and said, "I'm wondering if we shouldn't mop before we get to the dusting."

Heat raced into Eliza's cheeks, and she puffed them out in frustration. This uncoordinated person was not who she was. She jumped to her feet and held her hand out for a rag.

"We cleaning up this place so you can reopen?"

Travis gave her a quick glance as he handed her the window spray and rags, then busied himself with the mop bucket. "Something like that."

## 4

Travis was regretting taking Isaac up on his offer of the volleyball player's help. He'd needed someone, though, and she was the only one Isaac had been able to come up with off the top of his head. That, and she was apparently a hard worker. Reliable. She often helped Isaac and his wife at the bed and breakfast when things got too crazy during tourist season.

But still. There had to be a guy somewhere in town that could use a few hours of work. Someone who was strong and could help move heavy boxes around in the back room. Someone...less distracting.

Travis placed himself on the opposite end of the store to the volleyball player and told her it would be better if they both started at the outside and worked their way in as they cleaned windows and dusted.

Really, he just needed space.

And he knew the beach volleyball player type. The bubbly, outgoing, I'm-on-a-natural-high kind of woman who never stopped talking. They were always fantastic kissers, but Travis was no longer interested in that particular perk. Just one of many reasons he needed to keep this one at a distance.

"I'm Eliza, by the way," she called across the store. "I guess you already know that from when we met earlier, though."

He should have known, but he didn't want to admit that he'd forgotten her name within five minutes of their meeting.

A pause.

"So, Davis is in Thailand, huh? I've never been, but I've always wanted to. I bet it's beautiful. I've never really been anywhere, though, so there's that."

Eliza certainly ticked the I-can't-stop-talking box. Travis began dusting the power tool shelf for the fourth time. "Yup."

"That's awesome he has a girlfriend. Isaac told me. What's she like?"

This one-sided conversation had taken a sharp turn into I'd-rather-be-dead-than-talk-about-that-with-you.

So he didn't answer.

"Come on, I have to know." Eliza paused and glanced back at where Travis had moved on to the plumbing aisle. "Up until recently, Davis had lived here his entire life, and I don't think he ever went on a date. Not once. I'm interested in what his type is."

Travis released a long sigh. "Bald. Handlebar mustache. Likes to ride motorcycles."

Eliza pumped one fist in the air. "I knew it!"

Travis fought a smile that tried to break through. Maybe Eliza wasn't completely terrible, and she was helping the work go by quickly. Isaac had been right, she was efficient. But after only two hours, the time had come to cut things short. They had worked toward the middle of the store, and she was now scrubbing a shelf right next to him.

Travis tried not to notice the muscles in her arm that flexed as she cleaned. Or how she would bite her bottom lip when she scrubbed a particularly tough spot. Her eyes lit up whenever she thought of a new topic of conversation—one that she thought

Travis might enjoy. He felt bad—she was trying so hard. And all he could come back with were one-word answers.

But he couldn't allow himself to get too close. And the more Eliza chattered on, the more he found himself liking her.

"Thanks for your expert cleaning skills," he said, stretching and standing. "The windows and shelves look a thousand times better. I think I can probably take things from here."

Eliza glanced up as she finished the shelf she was on, surprised. "You sure?" She seemed conflicted, like she wondered if she'd done something wrong.

"Yeah, it will be easier to mop when I'm the only one here. And most of what I have left is moving a few heavy things around in the back."

Davis was flying in the next day to show him the ropes, and Travis wanted to leave a good impression. Show him that he could handle things. Show Davis that even though the man had stolen the woman he loved, Travis was all right. Better than all right.

A weight settled in his stomach. Travis didn't want to make sure that Davis knew he could handle it—he wanted Chloe to know. Wanted Davis to go back to Thailand and confirm that Travis was great. He was fantastic. Everything under control. The store couldn't be in better hands.

Because the only thing worse than Chloe rejecting him was her thinking he was heartbroken over it.

"I can move things," Eliza said, her voice breaking through his thoughts.

Travis rubbed his eyes, bringing himself back to the present. "Really, no need. They are very heavy, and with a dolly, I'll be fine."

In truth, there were a lot of boxes back there. Apparently, a shipment had arrived just before Davis had left, because the boxes had been unceremoniously thrown into the back, leaving little room to move. Davis would show Travis the ins and outs of sorting and scanning and doing inventory when he arrived, but Travis could at least move and stack the boxes and make things a bit more presentable.

All about the first impression.

"If I were a man, would you let me help?" Eliza asked, her eyes narrowing. Oh no, she was *that* type of athlete. The *anything you can do, I can do better* type.

Travis wasn't going to fall into it. "Look, you've been scouring this place for the past two hours. I just figure you're probably ready to be done for the day, and I'm happy to finish up." He reached into his back pocket to pull out his wallet and pay Eliza for her time, but before he had the chance, she'd brushed by him and was making her way into the back of the store.

"I see what you mean," she said when she'd reached the back room. "Do you want all the boxes stacked, or just against the wall? We could probably do two stacked, no problem, but with how heavy they are, I don't know if I'd stack them any higher. Don't want to damage the merchandise."

Travis grumbled under his breath. The woman was overcompensating now, trying to sound like she knew what she was talking about. Trying to prove something. And she was going to injure herself in the process. "Really, you don't have to—"

His words were cut short when Eliza lifted one of the heavier boxes and placed it on another in the far corner. And then she squatted, the muscles in her thighs taut, and did another. These were boxes that Travis would have used a dolly for, and here she was, lifting them like it was no big deal.

"Do you lift weights?" he asked. And then realized what a ridiculous question that was. Of course she lifted weights. No one was naturally that strong.

Eliza placed another box and gave a quick nod. "Used to do it competitively but got bored. I still lift a couple of times a week, though. I don't want all that work to go to waste."

So, the chattering athlete wasn't just a volleyball player. That was intriguing.

"Anything else you compete in that I should know about?"

After lowering herself behind a box and pushing it across the floor to a far wall, Eliza straightened and gave him a small smile. "No. But if you're curious, I get antsy and switch sports every couple of years. After the volleyball competition in a couple of months, I think it will be time to move on. Haven't decided what to, though." She paused and wiped her forehead with the back of her hand. "You going to help me or just watch me work?"

Heat rushed into Travis's cheeks, and he turned toward the box nearest him. "Of course. I just wanted to make sure you were up to it."

Eliza smiled, like she knew he was full of crap, and wheeled the dolly toward him.

Nope. If Eliza didn't need one, neither did he. And to prove it, he squatted low and lifted the box.

"I don't think that's a good idea," she said, a worried expression replacing her smile. "Maybe..." Her words trailed off as he straightened. She took a step forward as if to take the box from him, but he shot a scowl her way. She stopped and took a step back.

Oh gosh, this was heavy. Too heavy for him to be doing this. But Travis was known for being strong. He was the one that everyone had come to on the worksite in Thailand if they'd needed help with something heavy.

Everything else had been taken from him, and now this too?

Travis wasn't about to let Eliza out-lift him. Even if she could obviously lift three times what he could. Now that he was paying attention, he saw how huge her thighs were.

Not that he was looking. Just a casual observation.

Travis tried not to grimace as he took a step. Nope. He was losing grip. It was too much. He tried to set the box down, but he must not have done it right, because he felt something pull in his back. Or maybe it had snapped. Because pain shot through his entire body, and the box came crashing to the floor.

Eliza was immediately kneeling at his side. "Where does it hurt?"

Travis couldn't respond for a few moments. The pain was too great. "Everywhere," he finally choked out.

"You need an icepack to help reduce swelling." Eliza stood. "Do you have a freezer? I have some compression bandages you can use after."

Irrational anger boiled inside Travis. And hot shame. Hadn't Eliza done enough? She'd already proved herself more capable than him, and now she had to see him writhing on the floor because he couldn't lift a stupid box.

"I'm fine," he said, his voice low as he attempted to keep the anger from boiling over. He attempted to sit up, and more pain shot through his back. He couldn't hide the pathetic whimper that escaped his lips.

"You're not fine." Eliza extended a hand to help him up. "Where are you staying? Upstairs in Davis's apartment?"

Davis.

This was all his fault. If he hadn't ever left his stupid hardware store, he would never have met Chloe. Would never have upended Travis's life. And Travis wouldn't be on the ground, wishing he was anywhere but here.

"Yes, but like I said, I'm fine," he snapped. Travis immediately regretted it. It wasn't fair to take his frustrations out on

Eliza. It wasn't her fault that she was stronger than him. Or more capable. Or that Travis resented being there in Starlight Ridge at all. "Sorry," he murmured.

Eliza frowned but took his arm anyway and helped him to his feet. Once there, she slung one of his arms around her shoulders and supported his weight as they made their way up the back stairs. Every step felt like fire was shooting through his back and down into his legs, and they almost gave out on him several times.

Once they were inside, Eliza lowered him onto a worn couch in the living room—the only couch. She rummaged in the freezer and pulled out some meat that she handed him. Must have been Davis's, because Travis had yet to make it to the store since arriving that morning.

"You have pain medication?"

Travis slowly shook his head as he arched his back so he could slide the frozen meat against it.

Ouch.

Travis didn't have much of anything at all. Once he could walk again, he needed to visit the local market.

How long would it be until he could stand without having to fight back tears?

Eliza kept her distance, folding her arms across her chest. "I'll have Patty stop by with medicine." Though her words were kind, her tone was crisp. She was angry with him, which he deserved.

"I still need to pay you," Travis said, attempting to pull his wallet from his pocket, but another slice of pain stopped him.

"Consider it my housewarming gift," Eliza said, then she left, shutting the door harder than necessary on her way out.

So much for first impressions, Travis thought, as he was left with nothing to do but stare straight ahead at the closed door, nothing but pain for company. And the realization that he really needed to use the bathroom.

Travis wondered how long he could hold it.

And another thing...

Who was Patty?

## 5

Eliza fumed as she worked, moving the rest of the boxes that needed to be stacked. She didn't even know why she was bothering. The new hardware store manager was intolerable. He was distant and rude and ungrateful.

A bit like Davis had been. Except, Travis made Davis look like the gentlest soul in the world.

Eliza thought back to their time together. She hadn't slacked off, working the entire time, and now she'd even moved every single one of the boxes that Travis had insisted he could do himself.

Which made her realize exactly what this was.

An ego trip. He didn't like that she was stronger than him.

Eliza had seen it all before.

Her thoughts flitted back to Craig.

A pang settled in her chest, and she pushed it away.

No use crying over things she couldn't control—things that weren't anyone else's fault—things that just were.

Once the last box had been stacked, Eliza let herself out. She nearly locked the store's door behind her but then realized she didn't know if the back door was open. If not, Patty wouldn't be able to get in to tend to Travis.

That just riled up more anger. She pulled out her phone and dialed Patty, the town doctor. Better that someone else deal with the newcomer. Eliza would have to remember to tell Isaac not to volunteer her for any more jobs.

Of course, Patty was thrilled that she'd be able to meet the man she'd heard so much about—the man who'd only been in town for a few hours. Eliza shoved her hands into her pockets and walked the boardwalk, making her way home.

On the way, Eliza managed to meet at least six people who were on their way over to the hardware store, all with welcome baskets cradled in their arms. Everyone wanted to be the first to find out if it was true that Davis had managed to snag himself a girlfriend and moved halfway across the world. The first to meet the new guy. The first to see if he was as handsome as they had heard.

Good. They could have that honor. Because Eliza wanted nothing to do with Travis and his stupid store and his stupid hurt back.

Eliza had no reason to feel guilty about any of it, because Patty was on her way, and with all the baskets Travis was receiving, it wasn't possible for the man to starve while he was waiting for his back to heal.

She hoped Travis wasn't as rude to the others in town as he had been to her. They didn't know he'd been injured. And even if they had known, it wouldn't stop them from wanting to make sure he was well taken care of. It wasn't because they were trying to be nosy or intrusive—they just really cared. And yes, she could admit, curiosity played a part. Travis was just going to have to get used to it.

Eliza was nearly home when she realized she'd left her exercise bag at the hardware store.

Great.

At least it was just inside the store, next to the door. She could get in and get out with no one being the wiser. Eliza spun around, and twenty minutes later, she once again stood in front of the hardware store. Seemed like the welcoming committee was either all upstairs or had already dispersed because, thankfully, no one was around.

She stepped into the store, grabbed her bag, and was out before anyone saw. Or so she thought.

An arm slipped through Eliza's as she turned back toward home, and suddenly Jessie was walking beside her, strolling the boardwalk as if it were completely natural that the older woman had materialized out of thin air.

"Beautiful day, isn't it?" Jessie asked, taking a long, slow breath, relishing it all.

Oh, dear. This couldn't be good.

Sure, Jessie looked all innocent to anyone who wasn't a native of Starlight Ridge, but that was when Eliza needed to be the most cautious.

The woman was up to something.

"Sure is."

It was silent as they walked past Adeline's chocolate shop. Looked like Eli was on break from filming because he was in there helping set out chocolates. How Adeline had managed to snag a famous movie star and convince him to settle down in Starlight Ridge of all places, Eliza would never know.

"I just delivered a welcome basket to the handsome fellow taking over for Davis," Jessie said.

Here they went. This was where Jessie had been wanting to steer the conversation.

"Oh, did you?" Eliza asked.

Jessie gave a vigorous nod. "Yup. First one there."

"Were not," a voice said from behind them. Erwin. Of

course he was right behind Jessie. He usually was. "I got there first, and you know it. I'm always first, but you never give me the credit."

Jessie waved her hand through the air like he was an annoying fly she didn't know what to do about. "I arrived at the store first but stopped to see what a lovely job Travis had done in cleaning the place. Erwin swooped past me, up the stairs—he's quite quick for someone his age, you know—and happened to get to the apartment just ahead of me. But it was all very underhanded."

A harumph from Erwin.

Those two were constantly bickering, and yet they couldn't leave each other alone. It was as if they had found their life purpose in frustrating each other.

"As I was saying," Jessie continued. "Poor guy was moving boxes before we got there. Davis arrives tomorrow, you know. Anyway, Travis hurt his back, the poor dear. Patty got him all set up, but it could be a couple of weeks before he's really able to move as he wants to."

Eliza couldn't stop the humorless snort that escaped. Travis moving boxes? Of course he wouldn't want to set the record straight. From the sound of it, he had completely erased Eliza from the narrative, leaving only him and his heroic efforts to get the hardware store back into shape before Davis's arrival.

"What was that, dear?" Jessie asked, raising an interested eyebrow.

Eliza gave a small cough. "Sorry, it was nothing. Allergies." Which wasn't a complete fabrication. All that dust from inside the store had set her sinuses on fire.

"It's a blessing I was there, you know," Jessie said.

They were rounding the street corner and making their way towards Mueller Market and the florist shop. Eliza wondered how far Jessie intended to walk with her. They'd already passed

Jessie's home, and they'd lost Erwin back at the end of the boardwalk.

"Yes, I'm sure Travis will enjoy your tarts. Everyone does."

Jessie gave an absentminded "mm-hmm," her mind seemingly elsewhere. "You know, visiting with that nice young man, it got me thinking."

Eliza was sure it had. Anything that involved a new single young man got her thinking. Not for her, of course. But in addition to being the town baker and gossiper and head of the welcoming committee, Jessie was also the resident matchmaker. Or at least she liked to think of herself as one. Whether she was actually good at it was another thing entirely.

Eliza didn't respond, grateful she was almost home, but Jessie didn't seem to mind.

"Every year, thousands of tourists come visit our home, correct?"

Oh, this was taking a different turn than Eliza had been expecting. "Yeah..."

"And they bring a lot of money into our community, right?"

Couldn't argue there.

Jessie's expression had lit up, and she was talking faster now, whatever vision she had in her head seemingly threatening to explode out. "The county hasn't been giving us the budget our town deserves, always sweeping us to the side. What if we were able to raise money ourselves?"

And now Jessie had lost her. "I'm not sure I understand. What are we raising money for?"

Jessie unhooked her arm from Eliza's and pulled her to a stop. Her eyes danced in excitement. "Travis was working for that service organization that Davis ran off to, right? They get other people to donate money so they can build homes for those who need it."

Eliza nodded, but then realized Jessie would think that

meant Eliza was following the older woman's train of thought. "You want to raise money to build homes?"

"Of course not. What would we need more homes for? This town has all the people we can handle."

Exactly what Eliza had been thinking.

Jessie released an exasperated sigh. "Don't you see?" She gestured toward the old library just across the road. It was falling apart, unusable, having suffered extensive water damage when Eliza had been a child. A huge storm had nearly taken it out, and there it had sat, broken and sad, ever since.

Because the storm had caused so much damage throughout town, they hadn't had the money to repair the library—homes and other buildings had taken precedence.

The derelict building had become somewhat of an icon, even though the residents of Starlight Ridge hadn't been able to check out library books for over two decades, and the idea of repairing it had dwindled until it wasn't more than an occasional thought.

"We can have a big event where we raise money to rebuild the library," Jessie said, her voice rising in excitement. "Everyone loves a good old-fashioned charity where they can feel good about themselves. And if we include the tourists, think of how deep some of those pockets go."

It actually wasn't a terrible idea. Eliza would love to see the old library rebuilt, but she still had her reservations. "Usually when you're on vacation, you don't want to worry about others —about charities. You're just there to have a good time."

Starlight Ridge didn't have the money to put on a big event like it seemed Jessie was thinking of, and if this thing flopped and the tourists didn't come with their wallets open, it could be a disaster.

Of course, it also wouldn't be the craziest thing the town had ever done. And that was one of the things Eliza loved most about the people of Starlight Ridge—the way they just charged forward and did things because they wanted to, even if it didn't always make logical sense.

"I want to hire you," Jessie said, taking Eliza's hands in hers. "I want you to help me make this event the best thing this town has ever seen. The tourists won't be able to help themselves. Especially if we get Eli involved."

So, it wasn't Eliza's love life, or lack thereof, that Jessie had been interested in—it was her skills. Her ability to do odds and ends. That was a relief. Because, really, that was what Eliza was best at—randomness. She was proficient at a lot of things but hadn't truly mastered anything. She knew just enough to get by and keep people happy. She could complain about not having truly reached her potential—and heaven knew she had complained—but there were always plenty of odds and ends to do around the town, and it paid the bills.

Even if this event was a total flop, at least they could say they'd tried, and Eliza would have fun while doing it. Working beside Jessie was always an adventure. And if Eli was involved, that did change things. Since he'd married Adeline, the owner of Starlight Chocolate Confections, Eli had become just another Starlight Ridge resident, but to everyone else, he was a famous movie star, and that would certainly draw a crowd.

"All right," Eliza finally consented. "How long do we have to plan this thing?"

That was when Jessie's smile turned simply devious. "We already have thousands of tourists who flock here when we celebrate the kickoff to summer. Why not have it then?"

Eliza's heart dropped, and her stomach felt queasy. "That's in three weeks."

"It sure is. We'll have a resident-only event the week before, then our big showcase on the following Saturday and Sunday. Which means we have some work to do."

Eliza wished she had asked the important questions at the beginning. Knowing that Jessie wanted this thing pulled together that quickly, she was now afraid to ask for details.

"What exactly are you proposing we do to raise money?" Eliza closed her eyes, preparing for the answer.

"For the residents, an auction. For the tourists, a private screening of Eli and Leanne's movie, *Amaretto*. Both Elli and Leanne can be there to do a Q&A after the screening. We could charge a ridiculous amount of money and do four or five showings a day."

Eliza opened her eyes. That wasn't so bad. Their very own Leanne, owner of the bed and breakfast, was the screenwriter for *Amaretto*—it was what had brought Eli to Starlight Ridge in the first place. Jessie's plan was actually genius.

"That's a lovely idea, Jessie. Do you think we need to have an auction, though? The private screenings will bring in the majority of the funds." Eliza didn't know what the residents of Starlight Ridge had to offer each other that could get them bidding very high at an auction.

Jessie patted Eliza's hand as she turned to walk back toward her own home. "Oh, the auction is necessary. We've never done one of those before, and I want it to be an annual event. A way to bring the community together. Everyone will be involved, even that handsome Travis fellow."

That piqued Eliza's interest. From what she'd seen that afternoon, he hadn't exactly seemed the type to get involved with small-town events. "What will he be contributing?"

Eliza would have thought something like a nice tool set, but judging from Jessie's smile, she knew it wasn't.

"That would ruin the surprise."

And then Jessie sauntered off as if she were thirty years younger and not sprouting gray hair, chuckling to herself as she went.

## 6

Travis tried to listen. He really did. But Davis was talking about computers and inventory and ordering and all sorts of stuff that Travis had never needed before, and it was too much all at once. In Thailand, if he'd needed supplies, he'd driven into town and visited local shops—talked to people. And then those people had taken his money, loaded what he needed in the back of a truck, and that was that.

It didn't help that whenever Travis saw Davis—whenever he even heard Davis speak—all he could think of was Chloe.

And how Travis's back was killing him—something that had never happened in Thailand.

Was he getting old? Was that it? Had his body just given out on him after working it so hard for so many years?

Travis's attention returned to the present when Davis asked, "You get all that?"

He ran his fingers through his hair. "Yup. Got it."

Davis raised a skeptical eyebrow. "Okay, you teach me, then. How do you do inventory?"

What was he, twelve? This was the kind of thing his teachers had tried to pull on him. He was too old for this—if thirty-three could be considered old. He'd certainly felt it these past couple of days.

When it was apparent that Davis wasn't going to let him off the hook, Travis released a sigh. "Inventory. You look at what you have, what you don't have, and what you need more of. Then you enter it into the computer, and you buy more."

Davis gave a sad shake of his head. "This is important, Travis. This store is important to my family."

"Then why aren't *you* here running it?" Travis's words came out angrier than he'd intended, the frustration of the past couple of weeks exploding out with them.

Davis didn't rise to the bait, instead remaining calm. "You know why."

Yes, Travis did know why.

What he didn't know was why he was there in Davis's place.

What had possessed him to accept the position?

He was here now, though, and if he ever wanted Davis to leave him alone, Travis would need to learn everything that Davis was there to teach him.

Besides, Travis had about thirteen welcome baskets awaiting him upstairs, just begging to be eaten, with another seven arriving later that evening, or so Jessie had told him. Tarts. Shrimp. Fish.

Jessie. That woman was everything he'd been told, and more. She was a younger and feistier and funnier version of his own grandmother.

And apparently his arrival had inspired her to begin working on a small-town auction to help raise money for the local library.

Travis still didn't understand how his presence had anything to do with that, but she insisted it did. He figured that if someone needed to take credit, might as well be him.

"I'm sorry, Davis. Things have been tough the last while for me," Travis said, settling in at the computer and giving his best apologetic smile. "I really am going to try, and I'll do your family proud."

Davis visibly relaxed, and a hint of a smile even appeared. "Thank you. I appreciate it. And don't think I didn't notice how great the store is looking. Seriously, you've done a fantastic job —it makes it difficult to believe you arrived only yesterday."

Guilt pricked at Travis; he knew almost none of that had been him. "I really didn't have much to do with it. You see—"

"Don't be so modest," Davis interrupted. "Jessie told me how much work you put into this place, and you even injured your-self while doing it."

Injured doing nothing was more like it.

"But that's the thing, I had—"

And then Davis was back to teacher mode and walking Travis through everything he needed to know.

And Travis let him, because the truth was far too embar-rassing.


It took a week, and Davis was relentless, but Travis managed to complete his training. Apparently, he was a model student. It wasn't any easier to be around Davis than it had been back in Thailand, but they'd managed to put aside their differences for a few days.

Now that Travis's back was beginning to feel better and he'd managed to make his way through the thirty-two welcome baskets he'd received, things were looking up. He had a roof over his head for the first time in six years, air conditioning, and an entire community who thought he was the most amazing thing to ever walk into Starlight Ridge.

Well, most of the community.

Travis hadn't seen Eliza since his first day in town. He'd

caught a glimpse of her at the beach, siting at the lifeguard station. She'd seen him too—and then quickly turned her head, pretending she hadn't.

Seemed that was the kind of terms they were on now.

It was better that way, he reminded himself.

But the rest of the community? Travis never had a moment to himself and was rarely inside the hardware store for more than thirty minutes at a time, which was a good thing. It had been what he'd been hoping for. Except, many times when Travis was called out on a job, he wondered if it was because the person really was incapable of the repair themselves or they just wanted an excuse to get him out there.

Not that he thought of himself as anything special—he wasn't that kind of guy. But it was hard not to let those thoughts creep in when the majority of the calls he received were from single women who needed a doorknob tightened (the screws had obviously been loosened) or a picture hung on the wall (apparently she couldn't reach, even though a ladder was leaning against the side of the house, just waiting to be used).

It was when Travis had been in town for nearly two weeks that Jessie came hurrying into the store, waving a flyer at him. The big auction the town was putting on. He'd noticed tourists beginning to trickle in, the quietness that he had appreciated when first arriving being replaced by a thrum of anticipation. Residents were preparing their shops for the big influx that would apparently happen the following week.

They said it was like a flash flood, where you could see signs that something was coming. And then BAM, the streets and hotels and beaches were flooded with newcomers, all excited to finally be free from school and jobs and out on the California beach.

Travis didn't think he had much to prepare for, because, well, he ran a hardware store. But he was told it would affect him too, just not in the ways he anticipated.

More people meant more things broken, and the residents would keep him busy from the beginning of June through the end of September.

Jessie handed him the flyer, a grin spreading from ear to ear. "You'll be there, right? This Friday night."

Travis hesitated as he looked it over. Dread settled in his stomach. All of this was a bit overwhelming. Jessie was using the local community center for the auction, and apparently the entire town would be packed in there. The thought of it—it was a lot. "Look, Jessie, I know it's going to be fantastic, and I'd be happy to purchase one of the items or just donate money, but I think I'm going to need to sit this one out."

Travis worried that his not wanting to attend the event would cause offense—that Jessie would spread the news that the new guy wasn't a team player. That he thought he was better than the rest of them.

But really, he was just burned out, socially. That wasn't a problem he'd thought he'd have in Starlight Ridge, but there it was. Everyone was so tight-knit, so involved in each other's lives, all Travis wanted was a night at home. Alone.

But Jessie didn't seem the least offended. In fact, she laughed. "Nonsense. If you stay home, how will people bid on what you're offering?"

Travis gave her a wary smile. "Is this your way of telling me that I forgot to donate something for the auction?"

Her smile only grew. "Not at all."

Travis leaned against the checkout counter. "Really."

Jessie gave a quick nod. "I know you've been busy getting settled and everything, and I wanted to help out where I could, so I took care of your donation for you. One less thing on your plate. But how would it look if you weren't there for the auction? I mean, really, it would make us all look bad, don't you think?"

Travis rubbed a hand over his face. Jessie had this sweet small-town woman act down, and she knew how to use it. Travis now felt guilty just thinking about not showing up. And even though he had no idea what he'd apparently donated, he felt like he had no choice but to give in.

When he didn't respond right away, Jessie added, "Besides, Eliza will be there."

Travis's breath hitched. "Will she?" He tried to sound like he didn't care one way or the other, but Jessie gave him a knowing smile. She had figured out exactly which button to push, hadn't she?

Travis tried not to like Eliza. And he'd unintentionally succeeded in getting her to dislike him, but there was still that little nudge that told him he'd like the chance to know her better. Jessie was still watching him, and he tried to cover the momentary lapse by continuing. "I assumed she would be, along with the entire town. You know who it would be nice to see is..."

He tried to think of a name. Any name. Had he really not remembered a single person who had brought him a welcome basket? Those things had taken up his entire kitchen. "Patty. I don't know what I would have done without her when I pulled my muscle last week. That woman is a godsend."

Jessie gave a slow nod. "Yes, Patty will certainly be there. Though she may not be as interested in what you are bringing to the table." She paused for a second. "Then again, she might."

She was doing it again, alluding to this donation she'd so thoughtfully put together for him. Must be something big. And something that Jessie knew Travis would never agree to.

"And what exactly will I be contributing on Friday evening? A few donated hours of handyman work or something like that? Because I don't know how Davis would feel about me giving away hardware. He might be okay with it, but I'd feel better if I were donating my time instead."

Jessie's smile morphed into something else entirely. Oh, she was still smiling all right, but it was akin to a mischievous toddler who was just waiting for her mother to leave the room so she could rule the roost. "Yes, something like that. All you have to bring is yourself, and I'll take care of the rest." She pulled a folded sheet of paper from her pocket, smoothed it out on the counter, then in tiny letters wrote his name and *service* next to it. "See you then," she said, folding the paper back up. "And don't be late."

Jessie gave him a little wave, then hurried from the store, more flyers to hand out, he was sure.

He looked out the store's front window and noticed Eliza standing on the boardwalk with Jessie. The older woman was pointing to the flyer, talking excitedly, and Eliza was nodding but seemed to be feigning interest.

Travis couldn't help but smile. Eliza would have to talk to him again sooner or later and let him apologize for his behavior; she couldn't avoid him forever.

## 7

E liza hung the last of her flyers on the front door of the bed and breakfast. Leanne didn't usually allow that kind of thing—said it made her place look like a post office. Next thing she knew, there would be people pinning up pictures of weight loss supplements, while others advertised that they would buy your home for cash, no questions asked.

But this was for a good cause, the rebuilding of the library, and Leanne herself, along with Eli, would be the draw for many of the tourists wanting to attend the private screening of *Amaretto*. When Leanne had written the screenplay for the movie, Eli Hunt, of all people, had decided he loved it enough that it became his debut as a producer. Not only that, but he'd gone so far as to film the movie in their small town. Ever since then, Starlight Ridge had attracted more and more tourists, all wanting to visit the chocolate shop that played an integral part of the movie.

The fact that Eli Hunt himself would be at the screening? Well, Eli was the whole reason they were in Starlight Ridge in the first place, wasn't it? It didn't used to be that way, but, although Eli spent a lot of time away filming, everyone knew that he'd made a home in the small coastal town, and everyone wanted the chance to get a glimpse of the movie star.

And now they'd have the opportunity to ask him questions.

Jessie's idea had been brilliant.

Eliza was still unsure why they were having the auction, though. Sure, it could be fun. Jessie would donate her tarts or some other baked good, which everyone would bid on. But those were something they could regularly purchase. Eliza herself was donating five hours of work, so that one would probably go quickly.

But really...why?

The tourists would bring in all the funds they needed to rebuild the library, she was sure of it.

Music burst from Eliza's phone as she walked down the steep drive that led back to town. She slipped it from her pocket and glanced at the screen.

Well, speak of the devil.

"Hi, Jessie."

"How are things coming with the flyers? Do you need more?"

Eliza jumped a rock in her path. "I just put up the last of them, but honestly, we've plastered the entire town. If people want to attend the movie screening, they'll be sure to find it."

Eliza could practically hear Jessie smile through the phone. "Lovely, dear. Just lovely." A pause. "I do have one last thing to ask of you. This will be the last one, I promise."

It always was.

"What can I do for you?"

"I've just been informed by Erwin that in these types of charity auctions, people want hard numbers—a monetary goal. It seems we need to actually know how much money it will take to rebuild the library."

Yes, that was how these things went. It didn't make sense to raise twenty thousand dollars for a project that would cost one million. Eliza had assumed that Jessie had already done the legwork, but that was what Eliza got for assuming.

"I'm afraid I don't know much about that kind of thing," Eliza told her.

Jessie chuckled. "Yes, I know, dear. But Travis would, considering his line of work. Please stop by the hardware store and ask him to visit the library. A rough estimate will do."

Eliza's pace slowed until she was at a complete standstill. "You want me to... Oh, I don't know if that's such a good idea, Jessie. Can't you call him?"

Being the resident handyman, everyone had his number. Well, except Eliza, and that was on purpose.

"Afraid not. I hate to put you out, but I'll compensate you for the inconvenience. Give me a call when you have a good round number."

And then the line went silent.

Eliza was very aware of the fact that Jessie hadn't said why she couldn't call Travis. But once Jessie had her mind set to something, it was impossible to steer her in another direction.

Knowing what lay ahead of her, Eliza slowed her pace and took the rest of the journey at a leisurely stride. With any luck, Travis would be out on a job and she'd be off the hook.

When she reached the hardware store, her heart settled in relief. The CLOSED sign was flipped on the front door.

He wasn't in.

Eliza turned to leave, nearly bowling over Travis in the process.

Aw, crap.

"Hi," he said. That was it. No smile, no follow-up. No apology.

She tried to keep her expression similarly neutral as she said, "I was just leaving," and then stepped around him.

"Did you need something?"

Her footsteps slowed. Yes, she did. Or Jessie did, at any rate. But now that she was here, she couldn't bring herself to do it. Couldn't ask him. Couldn't even spend another minute with the guy. Eliza wanted nothing to do with him.

Which was why she was so annoyed with herself when she abruptly turned and asked, "Why does everyone act like you are a town hero?" She hadn't meant to say anything, but the way he'd treated her at his shop that first day still made her blood boil, and now seemed as good a time as any to let it all out.

Travis raised an eyebrow. "I'm going to need more to go on than that."

"Everyone thinks you're so good-looking, and so kind, and so amazing at what you do. The story that's going around is that you apparently swooped into town, cleaned the entire hardware store, and moved all those heavy boxes in one day, because you didn't want the town to have to go even a minute longer than necessary without their resident handyman and the supplies they needed, even at the expense of injuring yourself in the process. But you are too hard a worker to let that keep you down, or so people say. According to them, you are everywhere you are needed. If even so much as a nail comes loose, you are the first person people call." She paused, her breaths heavy. "You aren't that great. That day that you apparently did all that stuff? You were rude. And you can't even admit that I did most of that work. You took the credit. And I know I was getting paid to do it. You hired me. But still—you're a fake."

Travis stared—speechless.

Eliza threw her hands in the air and spun away. As she stalked off, she called over her shoulder, "Oh, and since you're so amazing, Jessie would like you to visit the library and tell her how much it will cost to rebuild. Says she needs an exact amount. Down to the penny." And then she hurried away before he could stop her.

That had felt good.

Sort of.

Not as good as she'd hoped it would.

Were all those things true? The unkindness that she'd slung at him?

Sure, Eliza was annoyed about how he'd treated her that day —like he should have been the one to do the heavy lifting; she had just been there to dust the shelves. And then Travis getting angry when he obviously couldn't.

She could admit, that was typical of male egos.

For him to take the credit of actually doing it, though—that was what had stung. Because honestly, Eliza would rather have Travis's job. Everyone in town knew they could hire Eliza to do random jobs. She was their miscellaneous woman. But people always wanted her to do things like passing out flyers or cleaning or watching their cat while they were out of town.

Watching someone's cat took zero work. Food and litter box. That was all they needed.

Maybe that was it. Eliza needed a challenge. And she'd finally been presented with one—one that used skills that were unique to her.

And no one even knew about it, because they all thought Travis had done it.

"Aargh, it's so annoying," she yelled at the sky as she rounded the corner at the end of the boardwalk.

"What's so annoying?"

Eliza stopped dead in her tracks. *Please, don't say he followed me. He can't have followed me.*

She turned around, and sure enough, there Travis was.

He had followed her.

"You adding stalker to your resume?" she asked, folding her arms over her chest.

Travis nodded toward a point up the road. "You said Jessie

needs an estimate on how much it will take to rebuild the library, and it sounded urgent. So I was going to the library. Which is up this road. Thought I'd hurry and get that done before I got another call from someone who needs a toilet repaired, which will miraculously start working again right when I get there." He frowned, like he was reliving a bad memory.

Eliza supposed she wasn't the only one in town who wasn't having their skills utilized. She straightened and lifted her chin. "Yes, it did sound urgent. And don't forget, it needs to be down to the penny."

Travis's frown deepened, like he didn't enjoy the prospect of that. "I really can't come up with a number that precise—I'm not a contractor. But I can give a ballpark estimate based on what I know."

Eliza released a heavy sigh. "I suppose Jessie will have to make do with that."

"Which is what she asked for in the first place." Travis's lips twitched up at the corners. "I called her right after you left to ask a couple of clarifying questions. Seems like you took some creative liberties when relaying her message." He paused. "You really hate me that much, huh?"

Hate? That was such a strong word.

"Not hate. Dislike? A little bit. Distrust? Absolutely. I don't know you."

Travis glanced at his phone, then started walking again. "You haven't even tried."

"Yes, I did. At your shop." Eliza quickened her steps to catch up, then matched Travis's pace. "You placed me on the complete opposite side of your store, like you couldn't get far enough away, you refused to answer any of my questions, and then when I out-lifted you, you told everyone in town that you had done all that work. Work that I never even got paid for."

"You said it was a housewarming gift," Travis reminded her.

"I only said it because you were writhing in agony. It was a gift that you were supposed to politely refuse."

Travis seemed to be fighting a smile. "I'm sorry, I was unaware of the protocol in that particular situation. Let's take care of that right away."

He stopped and reached into his pocket, but not without a flicker of pain crossing his face. His back must not have completely healed yet, and he'd been working with it like that for the past week.

"You really should be taking it easy, letting your muscles get the rest they need," she said, reaching for the money but then hesitating. It seemed wrong to take it now. Eliza pulled her hand back. "I don't want it."

"I insist."

Eliza met Travis's gaze and held it, no matter how badly she wanted to look away. "So do I."

And just like that, it had become a battle of endurance.

Travis's arm remained extended toward her, and he waved the money as if to say, *Aren't you going to take it?*

She folded her arms and set her mouth into a firm line.

He raised an amused eyebrow and smirked.

The battle was short-lived as she blew out a frustrated breath and said, "Ugh, fine." She took the money and slipped it into her back pocket. "And thank you."

It had been easy to be annoyed with him when he hadn't paid for her services. It was harder now. Especially because she knew he'd probably only survived the past week thanks to painkillers.

"I've seen you running around town working for Jessie, among others," Travis said. "No rest for the wanted." He threw a cocky grin her way.

"Yeah, dead or alive," she mumbled under her breath.

Travis released a laugh that sounded like a cannon had gone off, and she couldn't fight a small smile from breaking through.

"Careful, you're going to scare off the wildlife."

"I don't see you running."

Oh, ho! He could deal it as well as receive it.

She supposed she'd deserved that one.

Eliza pretended to be mad anyway, throwing a scowl his way. They were just approaching the dilapidated library, and she nodded toward it. "There's your next project. Have at it."

Travis hesitated, not crossing the road straight away. "How safe is that thing? I'm used to building from the ground up. Like, if I walk inside, is the entire thing going to cave in on me?"

That was something Eliza hadn't considered and was now wondering the same thing. As much as she didn't want to like Travis, she also didn't want him to die. "You know, it was shut down because of a massive storm, which probably means mold and mildew and all sorts of unpleasantness. Maybe you should start with the assumption that it could come down at any moment."

Travis gave a small nod as he considered the old building from afar. "We'll need to tear the whole thing down and start again."

"Does that drive up the price?" Eliza asked, worried what that would mean for their fundraising attempts.

"Not necessarily. Realistically, it probably reduces costs." He dug up the courage to walk across the road and get a closer look but didn't go inside, instead opting to peer through broken windows as he moved around the perimeter.

Curious, Eliza followed him across the road.

He glanced back at her. "A building this size, as long as you don't go high-tech, shouldn't be too bad. It's essentially a gutted-out home with some dividers and a bathroom."

"That sounds...awful." The images Eliza was having were

not of a library people would want to come and visit. "It's supposed to be inviting, with cool nooks for people to read in, an area for story time for the kids, and maybe even a computer lab. We could hold classes and—"

Travis held up a hand to slow her down. "Whoa, whoa, whoa. I get that a lot of libraries have that, and they are super artsy and big and have all sorts of resources. But we're talking about Starlight Ridge here. You need to have the funds for upkeep and to pay a librarian. And enough visitors to justify it all."

Eliza knew he was right, but she really didn't want to admit it. "You want to turn this place into a prison. I suppose the bathrooms will have communal showers and urinals as well?"

Travis lifted a shoulder. "Naturally."

"Awesome. Let me know how well that goes over at the next community council meeting."

Travis nodded as if he were seriously considering it. "I'll plan on it. When's the next one?"

"It was last night, which is when they agreed to move forward with Jessie's plan for the fundraiser, contingent on receiving an estimate of how much money the town needed to raise."

Travis hemmed and hawed, moving his fingers in front of him like he was doing calculations that only he could see. "Taking into account the communal urinals, and the petting zoo that I know you'll be asking for next, I'd say about three million."

Eliza gawked. "I'm sorry, how much?" There was no way the town would ever be able to raise that money, even with Eli Hunt and Leanne drawing a crowd.

"Without the petting zoo, cutting out the showers and including only one urinal, you might be able to get it down to five hundred thousand."

Aargh, that man was frustrating.

Eliza rubbed her forehead. "That's still a lot of money."

Travis looked over the building. "Like I said, it's a rough esti-mate. I haven't talked to contractors. I'm just using what infor-mation I've gathered over the past week from working with wholesale suppliers. And depending on what you're willing to go without, we could bring the cost down."

She nodded and attempted to look hopeful, even though it felt like her heart lay in the gutter.

Eliza had a lot of memories that she'd buried until Jessic had suggested they rebuild the library—good memories, but ones that Eliza didn't like to dwell on. Because they always led to Eliza asking, *Why?* And, *What if...?*

And now Travis was telling her they needed to raise half a million dollars if she was going to finally find some closure.

"I have to go," Eliza said, hurrying away from him and toward home. She didn't dare look back, because if she did, he'd see the panic that had settled in her chest. The fear. The desperation.

What she needed was a run. The type that made her lungs burn, and that made it impossible to feel anything else.

# 8

Travis leaned over the keyboard in his office, punching in numbers as Davis had taught him to. He didn't love this part of the job, but it also wasn't as awful as he'd thought it would be. If he were cooped up in the store all day like he'd originally assumed, then it would pose a problem. But a temporary reprieve wasn't bad.

Travis heard the front door to the hardware store open and then close. He stood, stretching, unsure how long he'd been sitting. When he entered the store from the back room, he saw Jessie browsing one of the aisles. She didn't see him but picked up a ratchet and feigned interest in it.

"That's a good brand," Travis said with a small smile. "I can ring you up, if you're ready."

Jessie glanced up, startled, then hurriedly put the ratchet back in its place. "Oh, no, just window shopping."

"Next time, then."

"Next time," she agreed. "Really, I was just stopping by to see if you'd had the chance to visit the library."

Travis pulled out his phone and scrolled through his sent messages. "Yeah. Did you not get my text earlier?"

Jessie laughed. "Honey, I have never sent a text in my life. I know that all these older people are trying to get with the times and pretend they know what they're doing with texting and video chat and all that, but I've never needed anything other than a nice old-fashioned phone call. Besides, a nice walk down the boardwalk is just what I needed this afternoon."

Travis slipped the phone back into his pocket. "I'm sure you probably know that the library needs to be demolished and rebuilt from scratch."

Jessie released a heavy sigh. "Yes, I was afraid of that. So, what's it going to cost us?"

That was such a difficult question with so many variables, and yet he was expected to know the answer because he knew how to fix leaky toilets and holes in drywall. "Look, I'm not a contractor. There are a lot of different people you're going to need to get estimates from if you want this professionally done."

Jessie walked over to him and placed a hand on his. "How much, Travis?"

He removed his hand and rubbed an eyebrow. "Without donations, if you keep it simple, you can probably do it for five hundred thousand, and that's just for the building itself, no high-tech fancy stuff. You should consider donations for things like books and shelves and interior design kind of stuff."

Jessie nodded slowly. "That's a lot of money for something we want to provide the community for free."

For a brief moment, he noticed the perpetual twinkle in her eyes had faded, but then it returned just as quickly. She hit her palms on the checkout counter and said, "We have the manpower, and the way. Flyers are up all over town, tourists are trickling in, and they are already calling to reserve their seats for the movie screenings. A hundred dollars per ticket is what we're charging, and people aren't even batting an eye. Not when they get the chance to sit in a Q&A with Eli Hunt."

"That means you aren't charging enough. A hundred dollars was your early bird pricing. Tomorrow, raise the price of the remaining tickets to two hundred."

Jessie scrunched up her nose, like she didn't think much of that idea. "That seems kind of sneaky, don't you think? And greedy?"

"It's economics."

"Economics sounds kind of underhanded to me," she said, her noise still scrunched up. "I don't want to raise prices from under their feet like that. Even if we don't know these people, our tourists keep the town running smoothly. We have to treat them right—treat them like family."

Travis sucked in a long breath, wondering how best to explain this to dear, sweet old Jessie. Because she did need to understand the financial aspect of all this if they were going to raise the money the town required for their library.

"Jessie, you have a product that you are offering—a special screening and the chance to meet Eli Hunt himself. The opportunity for fans to ask him questions. For some people, that's priceless. Right now, at a hundred dollars, they are buying it up quick, no thought required. You only have a limited number of seats and screenings, right? Sure, if you double the price, some people might drop out that would have otherwise bought a seat. But you'll still have people buying those tickets—people who are happy to pay the higher price. You'll still sell out, and you'll make twice as much money as you would have otherwise."

Jessie nodded slowly, her nose a bit less scrunched than it had been. "Yes, that makes sense. It still makes me feel like I'm taking advantage of good folk, though."

Travis placed his arms on the counter and leaned forward, looking Jessie in the eye. "I know you do. But you have to remember, you are raising money to help your town, not for your own gain. And people are happy to spend more money than they would normally if it's for a charity—if it's doing some good. And it will be. Communities need libraries. Children need a safe place to go and read and learn about the world around them. Adults needs books just as badly, and for many, it is the only way they have access to a computer. Computers allow them to connect with others, find jobs, and research topics that are important to them. Honestly, I'm shocked you've gone this long without a library."

Jessie's nose smoothed out, and she smiled. "Thank you, Travis. You truly are something special, aren't you?"

He thought back to Eliza's words, about how everyone thought he was so amazing. And how bitter she'd been about it. She'd called him a fake—a fraud. And maybe he was. "I don't know about that."

"Oh, no need to be modest. You're good-looking, hardworking, and humble. The complete package."

"I have to tell you, Jessie, I'm doing my best, but I couldn't have done it without help. Did you know Eliza helped me get the store ready when I first arrived? She did most of it, actually. Even moved all those boxes back there that were too heavy for me to handle."

The words hurt as he said them, but he didn't let his smile drop. It was hard. Being the strongest in town was what he'd always taken pride in. Now that a beach volleyball player, of all people, had outshone him, he needed to figure out what he did have. What made him special. What he could contribute, other than knowing how to use a hammer and a wrench.

Jessie matched his smile. "I know, dear."

"You do?" He must have looked as shocked as he felt, because Jessie laughed and moved toward the front door.

"I know everything, Travis. And as capable as you are, you're no match for our Eliza."

And then she left.

And as he sat in his office, slouched in his chair, trying to work, he was unable to keep his mind on the numbers in front of him.

Travis was no match for Eliza, huh?

He'd see about that.

## 9

Eliza set up the last of the chairs and looked around the community center. It didn't get used as much as it should and had become outdated. Everything about the place screamed 1970s, but when you lived in Starlight Ridge and had unlimited access to that beautiful ocean and a sky that looked like it could go on forever, why have your yoga class inside some stuffy old building? Not when you could be out on the sand, the wind in your hair.

For the purpose of the auction, however, they'd needed an indoor location. A built-in stage sat at the front of the large room, once-majestic drapes tied at the sides. She'd placed a few potted plants around the edges of the room, and a large home-made sign had been draped across one of the walls. *1st Annual Starlight Ridge Community Auction*, it said.

Jessie wanted this to become a recurring event, a chance for the community to come together and serve one another—not like they didn't already. But Eliza had to admit, she was excited for it. Everyone in town was donating either an item or a service. Some of the items would be part of a silent auction that would take place along the back of the room, but most would be up for bid, front and center on that stage.

Eliza smiled. She knew she was being paid to help out, but she was proud of what she'd done, and it felt good to be a part of the way the town was changing and adapting, becoming better. Starlight Ridge hadn't lost its small-town charm, but they were growing. It was a good thing. And this library would be just the start of it.

If only she could get this dumb headache to go away. It had appeared that morning, but with some well-timed pain medication and lots of water, she'd been able to keep it under control.

From the way the pain was currently grinding at her temples, it was time for another dose.

"Oh my goodness, it's beautiful," Jessie said, walking into the room. White Christmas lights had been strung across the ceiling, because that was all Eliza had been able to find in the community center's storage closet. It suited the mood, though, and she could admit it made for a stunning addition.

"Thanks. You don't think it's a bit much?" She knew it wasn't, but she wasn't above fishing for compliments.

Jessie spun in a circle. "Not at all."

Eliza smiled, but then her smile dipped. Her headache was suddenly much worse, and she wasn't feeling so good. Nausea. Room spinning. Where was her water? Had she drunk it all? A quick glance around the room told her it wasn't there. She must have finished it.

She held out a hand to steady herself but wasn't quite successful.

"Are you all right, Eliza?"

She could hear Jessie but didn't answer. Nothing was as important in that moment as finding a toilet. Couldn't puke all over the newly decorated room, not with the auction only two hours away. She stumbled out of the room and down a hallway until she reached the bathroom.

Twenty minutes later, she trudged out, her body drenched with sweat.

Jessie had been waiting right outside the door. "Oh, my dear, I'll get you home. No auction for you this evening."

Disappointment settled in Eliza's stomach. She'd been looking forward to this so badly—you could only have one inaugural event, after all. And she'd helped plan it and decorate. And she wouldn't even be there to bid.

Eliza had seen the list of items, and there were some good ones on there.

"I wanted to bid—wanted to support people. And the library," she mumbled, allowing Jessie to lead her away. Her face felt like it was on fire.

Jessie patted her hand. "I've pushed you too hard this week. Always have to have my big ideas and drag everyone else along with me."

"It was a brilliant idea." Eliza slipped away from Jessie and melted into a plush armchair by the front door. "Maybe I'll just sleep it off here." She nestled further into it. How had she not known how comfy this thing was? "Wake me when things are about to start."

A sigh. "You're in no state to walk home. I better get my car." A pause. "No wandering off, you hear?"

Why was this chair so comfortable? What had they filled it with, pillows?

"Did you hear me, Eliza? No wandering off."

Must be pillows.

And then Eliza closed her eyes and drifted off into a restless sleep.

. . .

ARMS AROUND HER, lifting. The sound of a car starting. More arms. Softness. She must be back in that delightful chair because she felt the pillows again.

"You sure she's okay?" A man's voice drifted through the fog.

"Patty is going to check in on her on her way to the auction but said it sounds like the flu."

Then some mumbling.

The auction.

It was going to be fantastic, and Eliza couldn't wait to go. Just as soon as she finished her nap.

"It's going to go to the highest bidder," she mumbled. "That's me. The highest bidder. I always win."

A pat on her hand. "Of course you will, dear. Of course you will."

"Two hundred dollars. That's what I saved up for tonight. We're going to rebuild the library. And I got two hundred dollars. I'm going to be the highest bidder."

The world went silent once more, and Eliza drifted back to sleep.


OCEAN WAVES. They crashed over her. No, that was the sound of her phone. Eliza's head still pounded, but at least the nausea was gone. She glanced at the time. Eight-thirty.

Eight-thirty. She was late for the auction.

Eliza tried to get out of bed, but her head swam, and she fell back into her pillow.

The ocean waves continued.

Eliza pressed the speaker button on her phone, and Jessie's voice filled the room, loud and clear.

"I'm sorry to wake you, dear, but I just had to be sure. You would like me to bid for you, correct? You told me you had two hundred dollars you were wanting to spend tonight. You wanted to be the highest bidder."

Why was Jessie speaking so loudly?

Eliza pressed her head against the pillow, hoping to dampen the noise. "Yes, Jessie, thank you. I'm sorry I'm not able to be there tonight."

"I understand, dear. I know you'd be here if you could. I see something particularly special on the docket for the evening. Would you like me try to win it for you?"

Eliza wondered if she had any painkillers in the bathroom cabinet. "Don't just try, Jessie. Give it all you got. I may not be able to be there tonight, but that doesn't mean I need to come away emptyhanded."

Jessie chuckled. "Right you are. Rest up, and I'll visit in the morning."

"Thanks, Jess."

After hanging up, Eliza realized she'd already forgotten what she'd asked Jessie to bid on on her behalf. Must have been something good, because all Eliza could remember was that it was something particularly special. She couldn't wait to see what it was.

Now, about those painkillers.

W hen Travis arrived at the community center early to deliver a few extra chairs, he hadn't expected to see Jessie half-dragging Eliza from the building. A car sat next to the curb with its door open.

"What's going on?" he asked, dropping the chairs he'd been carrying and jogging over.

"The poor woman was helping me decorate for the auction one minute, the next she's puking her guts up in the bathroom. I think I've pushed her too hard."

Travis highly doubted that. Eliza pushed herself harder on a daily basis than anyone else ever could. He slid in next to Eliza and lifted her in his arms, relieving Jessie of her burden. Jessie was in good shape for a woman who was probably in her late fifties, but she wasn't in any position to carry another human being. She gave him a grateful smile as he helped settle Eliza inside the car.

"Mind coming with me?" Jessie asked. "I don't know if I can get her inside on my own."

Travis wondered if he should be taking Eliza to the doctor instead but agreed to help in any way he could.

Erwin was walking up the sidewalk at that moment, and his gaze took in the scattered chairs, then moved to where Travis had just laid Eliza on the back seat of the vehicle.

"What's happened?" he asked, his tone panicked as his steps quickened.

Jessie seemed almost annoyed at the man's concern. "It's fine, Erwin," she called as she opened the driver's door. "Eliza has a bit of a bug, and we're taking her home to rest."

"I'll call Patty and send her right over," Erwin said, pulling out his phone. "I hope it's nothing serious. I had meningitis once. Had to stay overnight in the hospital. Head was hurting so bad, I couldn't turn it. Could barely walk." He paused, his expression stricken. "You don't suppose it's meningitis, do you? Mine was viral, which was lucky. But bacterial? She could lose a leg. Or worse."

"Thank you, Erwin," Jessie said, waving a hand through the air. "But it's not meningitis." She slid into her seat and started the car, leaving Erwin standing there, still talking about the various complications that could arise if it was in fact meningitis.

"He means well," she said with a sigh as she drove. "But sometimes you just have to cut that man off or we'd still be sitting outside the community center, waiting for him to take a breath so we could get this girl home."

Travis glanced back at Eliza's clammy face. He hoped that Jessie was right that it wasn't anything serious—was clamminess a symptom of meningitis?

A phone call from Patty as he carried Eliza inside her house put his mind at ease, though. She said it was late in the season for flu, but she'd already seen two patients that day who had tested positive for it.

Liquids and rest were all the girl needed.

That was a relief.

Jessie led the way and directed Travis up a flight of stairs and down a long hallway, second door on the left. He felt strange being here, like he was intruding. He knew that Eliza didn't think much of him, and he doubted she would have invited him inside her home if she'd had anything to do with it.

But she was currently sleeping, her breaths coming more rapidly than he thought was normal, so there wasn't much Eliza could do about it.

"Just place her on the bed," Jessie instructed.

He did as he was told, allowing a small smile when he noted her comforter. Penguins with surfboards. He hadn't known they made those kinds of things queen-size. The walls were adorned with posters that seemed more up Eliza's alley. Photographs of her winning competitions, holding trophies that were most likely collecting dust in an attic somewhere.

There was only one picture in the room that wasn't related to an athletic competition. It sat on Eliza's nightstand. In the photo, she was a young girl, maybe about six, and she was playing at the beach with a man and woman. Her parents. They had to be, considering how they resembled her.

"You good to go?" Jessie asked, breaking through his thoughts.

"Yup." He threw another glance Eliza's way. "You sure she's going to be okay?"

Jessie turned an intense gaze on him. "I would never let anything happen to Eliza, auction or no auction. Besides, Patty's going to stop by on her way, just to check up on her. She's in good hands."

He gave a quick nod and allowed Jessie to lead him out.

Travis hadn't known how he'd be able to relax and have fun that evening, not after seeing Eliza in the condition she was in, but once he stepped into the community center, it was difficult not to be swept up in the excitement. From the moment he entered, sounds of laughter surrounded him. No one was sitting down, instead perusing the silent auction table and enjoying refreshments that had been set out along one of the walls.

It was at this moment that Travis realized how few people in town he'd actually met. There had to be at least a couple hundred people there already, and he only recognized a handful.

Travis paused mid-step, a sudden longing washing over him for the days when he had known every single person who surrounded him. When he had been with Building for Hope, there had been only twenty to thirty people at any given time. And he knew them all. Travis had also known the name of every local villager they were helping, the owner of the market he shopped at regularly, and the barber who cut his hair once a month.

Here?

Travis's gaze swept the room. Erwin was helping himself to some punch. Mitchel, a guy Travis had met a couple of days previous, was talking to Erwin animatedly, his hands flying through the air as he laughed. It seemed to be a hilarious story, but Erwin only rewarded Mitchel with a half-smile.

Mitchel had hired Travis to help with a back porch DIY project that had gone wrong. He'd wanted to do a project with his teenage son, who was now hovering by the brownies, but they'd had to call Travis when half of the elevated porch buckled and crashed.

"Okay, okay," Jessie said, sprinting up onto the stage and grabbing a microphone from its stand. "How's everyone doing tonight?" If Travis had half that woman's energy when he was her age, he'd be happy.

Jessie was met with hoots and hollers, and she rewarded everyone with a grin.

"Welcome to our first annual Starlight Ridge community

auction. There is a lot of good stuff coming your way, and you won't want to leave early. As a reminder, all the money we make tonight, minus what we are paying the caterer, will go toward the library fund."

"Aren't *you* the caterer?" someone called from the crowd.

"Why yes, I am. Thank you for asking," she said, not at all embarrassed by it. "Was there someone else you were expecting to make the best baked goods you've ever eaten?"

That got a laugh from everyone, and the show continued.

Most everyone else took their seats as the auction commenced, but Travis wasn't quite ready. As he browsed the items that were part of the silent auction, Patty came hurrying in through the double doors.

"What did I miss?" Her face was flushed from exertion.

"Just the best baked goods you've ever eaten," Travis said, nodding toward the refreshment table.

Patty bent over and held her knees. "Oh, good."

"How's Eliza doing?" he asked when Patty didn't immediately offer an update.

She straightened, her complexion nearly back to its usual color. "Resting, and miserable, but fine. She'd noticed a headache coming on earlier in the day, but with so much to do, she pushed through and didn't think anything of it. That's the problem with people, they think they don't have time to take care of their health."

"So, she just overdid it is all?" Travis was relieved it wasn't anything worse. Not that it was any of his business—he was just concerned about a fellow Starlight Ridge resident. No more than Jessie or Patty had been. The normal amount of concerned.

"Oh, it's definitely the flu," Patty said, her gaze scanning the room. Jessie had just pulled out a gift certificate for the tattoo place that doubled as a laundromat. "But she might have had a fighting chance if she rested every now and then. Give her a few days, and she'll be fine."

The flu. It wasn't great news, but it could have been worse. It could have been meningitis.

Travis turned his attention back to the stage. He wouldn't have taken the Starlight Ridge folks as the type who would get excited about tattoos, but the bidding escalated quickly until Erwin won with a five-hundred-dollar bid. According to Patty, that was a steal. But what on earth did someone like Erwin want with a tattoo?

A woman walked by a few minutes later with an armful of auction paddles. "Sorry, I didn't notice you two back here." She handed one to Patty, then another to Travis. Number thirty-eight.

"Bree, have you met our newest resident?" Patty asked.

"I haven't had the pleasure." Bree stuck out a hand. "But I feel like I already know you with the way this town has been talking. My husband and I own the scuba shop just a couple doors down from you."

"It's nice to finally meet you," Travis said, taking her hand. "I haven't had the chance to thank you for the welcome basket you left for me at the store. I'm sorry I wasn't there to accept it in person."

She waved a hand through the air. "I hear we've been keeping you quite busy since you arrived. Hopefully folks haven't been giving you too much trouble."

"Not at all." Not *too* much, anyway.

Patty's gaze had zeroed in on the refreshment table, and she threw them an apologetic smile. "Sorry to cut this short, but those brownies are calling my name. I'll see you two around." She then beelined toward the opposite side of the room, and Jessie mistook Patty's waving paddle as a bid.

"That's forty dollars for an ice cream cake from Mueller Market from Patty," Jessie called out.

"I'm not bidding," Patty called back. "Why would I bid on an ice cream cake when I'm lactose intolerant?"

"Rules are rules," Jessie said, gently chiding the town doctor. "Keep your paddle down if you don't want the item."

Luckily for Patty, a man held up his paddle and she was saved from purchasing the cake she wouldn't be able to enjoy.

Bree excused herself as she made the rounds, making sure everyone was taken care of. Travis turned back to the silent auction and wrote down a bid for a couple of items, including a romantic getaway at the bed and breakfast. He hadn't visited his parents for a couple of years and thought they might like a trip to Starlight Ridge for their upcoming anniversary.

Travis eventually made his way by the refreshment table, loaded up a plate, and slid into one of the few remaining seats near the back. The entire event was entertaining, though he was quickly outbid every time he raised his paddle. The minutes ticked on, and after a couple of hours, it seemed the novelty of the auction was wearing off and the residents of Starlight Ridge stirred in their seats, getting restless. The metal folding chairs weren't exactly comfortable, and Travis didn't blame anyone for being ready to call it a night.

As if sensing she was losing her audience, Jessie called out, "This has been an incredible evening, but I do have one more thing up my sleeve, so bear with me for just ten more minutes." She gave a dramatic pause. "Travis Matkin, our newest resident, has graciously given a donation for this worthy cause, and it's one you don't want to miss."

Travis had just been about to take one last walk by the refreshment table and was halfway out of his seat when Jessie made this announcement.

He froze, then immediately dropped back to his seat as if he could hide from the hundreds of eyes that were seeking him out.

"Travis, why don't you come up to the stage?" Jessie beckoned him forward, and with all those eyes on him, he felt like he had no choice.

Travis had hoped that Jessie had forgotten about him and his donation. The one she'd volunteered him for. He considered bowing out, though he didn't know how he'd manage to do it gracefully, considering the rest of the town had all contributed some type of good or service. Even Eliza had contributed five hours of work, and she wasn't even at the auction. Her five hours of service had gone for a hundred and fifty dollars—not bad at all.

Not wanting to give a poor impression when so new in town, Travis made his way toward the stage, attempting a proper smile as he made what felt like a very long walk.

Jessie beamed at him as he joined her on the stage, and he held up a tentative hand and gave a small wave.

"I know this is unprecedented," Jessie started, her words slow, like she was purposely dragging them out to build anticipation. "But this one is only for the single ladies in the group, so to the rest of you, make yourselves at home at the refreshment table so I don't have to take any of that food home."

Travis's stomach felt like it had flipped upside down, and panic settled in. "I had agreed to a few hours of handyman work," he muttered so only she could hear.

"No, I remember specifically that you said, 'a few hours of handyman work, or something like that.' I chose to focus on the 'something like that' part of the sentence."

Travis doubted what Jessie was about to announce would be anything remotely related to handyman work. "Meaning?"

"That your handyman services go beyond what lies in your

store. Have you ever repaired a broken heart before, Travis?" Jessie murmured.

Not only was Travis's stomach flipped inside out, but his heart had dropped as well. Had he ever repaired a broken heart before? No, never, including the one he still lugged around. Except his hadn't just broken—it had shattered.

"I'm afraid that doesn't lie within my expertise," he said softly.

"Looks like you're going to need to learn on the job, then." And then her small smile exploded into a grin as she announced into the microphone, "Get your wallets out, ladies, because our highest bidder tonight will win a date with Travis Matkin."

Aw, crap.

# 11

Travis went numb. This wasn't happening. It wasn't. A terrible dream. A nightmare. He'd wake up soon enough. But he didn't, and Jessie cheerfully handed off the mic to a man he recognized as the scuba shop owner. As she descended the stairs to an empty seat in the front row, he heard her say to someone in passing, "I don't want to miss out on this one."

Of course. She'd set the whole thing up, then wanted a front row seat to watch it all unfold. Implode might be a better word for it, because there was no way this thing would end well.

Heat filled his cheeks as he searched for an escape route. Leaving with his dignity intact would have been nice, but at this point, the chances of that happening were slim to none.

So he laughed, as if he found the whole thing hilarious—as if it were a joke. And then proceeded toward the stairs. Unfortunately, the scuba shop owner—Caleb, he thought it was—used that to his benefit.

"All right, ladies, you can already see Travis here strutting his stuff. He's probably about six feet two inches. Not sure how much those muscles of his weigh, but I know you want a night out on the town with this one."

Travis smiled, waved, and had gotten to the first step when Jessie stood and quickly walked toward him. She gently laid a hand on his arm and turned him back around as she whispered, "This is for the library, remember? How would it look if you backed out and we lost all that money that could have bought our children the books they so desperately need?"

"You set me up," he whispered back, more than just embarrassed at this point. He was annoyed. And slightly angry—which was hard to do with someone as sweet as Jessie. But he'd reached his limit with small-town interference, and he'd been in town for less than a month.

He threw a quick glance at Jessie and was met with a smiling woman who had no regrets.

"You're right. I did. But I knew you wouldn't do it otherwise, and there's someone who needs this date more than you don't want to do it."

And then she walked back to her seat, placed her hands in her lap, and raised her auction paddle.

Hers was the first bid at thirty dollars.

That was why Jessie had been pushing so hard—because she wanted to win this date with him? Apparently Jessie was a cougar, and no one had warned him about it.

He should have known.

No one was that sweet, or baked that well, without having something they were trying to hide. Of course, she wasn't trying to hide it now. Caleb motioned for Travis to walk back toward him, and with all eyes fixed on him, and at least three catcalls, Travis reluctantly returned to the stage.

It was for the library.

It was for the town.

A town that he apparently needed to escape as soon as he'd finished with his obligations, because this place was messed up.

Travis smiled and did a little turn, his arms out to his sides, to show that he could be a good sport. Even if his smile felt more like a grimace.

"That's more like it," Caleb said with a grin. "Do I see forty dollars? Yes, forty dollars to Brenda."

Looked like Jessie had some competition. But when Travis saw this Brenda woman standing up on her chair in the back row, he found himself hoping it was Jessie who would win this one.

It wasn't that Travis thought himself above someone like Brenda. He was sure she was a very nice woman, but she seemed a bit...eager.

She was older than him by at least a few years, and had long curly hair piled on top of her head. She must have used an entire bottle of hairspray on that thing. And that lipstick...wow. With that shade of pink—it was like a lighthouse beacon.

Brenda was practically jumping up and down on top of her chair—not exactly safe with these flimsy folding chairs—and waving her paddle in the air.

Caleb smiled in her direction. "Okay, Brenda, you are currently the winning bid. But you have to put your paddle down or you're going to start bidding against yourself. Unless you'd like to do that—the library would thank you."

"I wouldn't mind," she shouted from the back, and chuckles rippled through the crowd, but she then lowered the paddle.

A few other women Travis didn't know joined in on the fun but dropped out when it reached one hundred and fifty dollars. Women would pay that much just to go on a date with him?

He was flattered, but that didn't change the fact that he really wasn't interested in any of the women here. Anyone he met, he immediately compared to Chloe, and she always won out.

*It's just one date*, he had to tell himself. *It's for charity.*

It looked like Travis would be going out with Brenda after all as she bid one hundred and sixty dollars.

"All right. A date with Travis is going once, going twice…"

Jessie lifted her paddle for the first time since her initial bid. Travis had come to the conclusion that she'd only bid to get things going, but that didn't explain why she would be bidding one hundred and seventy dollars. That was a risky move if all she was trying to do was move the bid higher. Travis had been burned using that tactic in Monopoly more times than he'd like to admit.

Caleb didn't seem at all concerned by the older woman bidding for a date with Travis, but instead seemed delighted that the final auction item of the evening was taking such an interesting turn.

"And Brenda has been outbid by the lovely Jessie. Brenda, what do you say, you going to take it up to one hundred and eighty dollars?"

She hesitated, but then raised her paddle.

Holy cow. What was happening here?

Travis thought for sure that Jessie must be out of the competition now, but no, there went her paddle. And there went Brenda's. Both looked determined, their lips tight in concentration.

Travis had stopped putting on a show, watching as the bids flew back and forth. Even Caleb had stopped announcing, merely calling out the dollar amount each time a paddle flew up.

"Two hundred and sixty. Two hundred and seventy…"

At three hundred and forty dollars, Brenda's hand hesitated. She looked like she might lift it but then kept changing her mind. She was no longer jumping on top of her chair but was instead biting on her lip, like she was unsure what to do.

Finally, in an act of defeat, she stepped down and slumped into her chair, looking a bit worse for wear.

Travis couldn't help but feel a little sad for Brenda. Maybe he'd still ask her out on a date when he'd fulfilled his obligation with Jessie. That felt weird just thinking about it.

A date with Jessie.

Nope, repeating it didn't make it any better. Each time, it just felt weirder.

"Congratulations, Jessie." Caleb's voice rang out over the crowd as they chattered and laughed, all congratulating Jessie like there wasn't anything at all weird about it.

Travis approached the woman, who was surrounded by well-wishers.

"Yes, congratulations, Jessie. I didn't know you were so fond of me."

Jessie gave him a mischievous smile. "Of course I'm fond of you. I wouldn't trust the single women of Starlight Ridge with someone I thought was trouble."

Travis cocked an eyebrow and said slowly, "Single women... such as yourself?"

Jessie laughed and waved a hand through the air. "You are a handsome man, don't get me wrong, but I wasn't bidding on my behalf. You're a bit young for me, don't you think?"

Relief rushed through Travis, and he released a small laugh. "Maybe a little."

It was apparent the moment Jessie realized what Travis had thought because she leaned back in her chair, her laughter intensifying.

"Oh, no," she finally managed to say. "I have plans for that date that I just won."

## 12

Eliza blinked quickly as the morning sun sneaked through her curtains. How many days had she been in bed? Two? Three? More?

Her fever seemed to have broken and she was actually hungry, which was a good sign.

Grabbing a robe from her closet, Eliza made her way downstairs to the kitchen. Overripe bananas sat on the counter, begging to be made into bread, but they were definitely not edible in their current form.

Frozen waffles it was. She pulled the box out of the freezer and popped two into the toaster. As she waited for them to brown, she reached for the bottle of pain medication that she'd left out. She retracted her hand, realizing she was only reaching for it out of habit. Her headache was gone, her energy wasn't back a hundred percent but it was getting there, and she was ready to start living her life again. Even so, her legs still felt a bit shaky, and she leaned against the counter to help support her weight.

Eliza had vague recollections of Isaac texting the past couple of days and offering to cover her lifeguard shifts, as well as other texts from well-wishers around town.

Get-well baskets.

She just now remembered the texts informing her of the baskets that had been left on the front porch, but she'd not had the energy to go out and retrieve them. Pushing off from the counter, she stepped out into the sun, shielding her eyes from its rays. Was it always this bright?

Sitting on the front steps were several baskets of medicine and easy-to-prepare food.

As much as Eliza struggled with Starlight Ridge sometimes, this was home, and she knew she couldn't go anywhere else. No, she didn't have a full-time job, even though she had a college degree. It was from an online school, but still, a degree was a degree. It was in health studies, and she had thought of using it to continue on and become a physical therapist. That required a doctorate degree, though, and leaving Starlight Ridge just hadn't ever worked out.

She sighed, knowing she needed to call it what it was.

Fear.

Ever since her mom had died, Eliza had been ruled by it.

When her mom had passed away, that had been the wakeup call.

The one that had gotten Eliza moving. Which had, ironically, also caused her to become stuck—paralyzed.

Eliza shook the thoughts from her head as she lugged the baskets inside. Her waffles popped up, and she set the baskets down in the entryway, not having the energy to deal with both them and breakfast.

She threw her waffles onto a plate, sucking in a quick breath and shaking out her fingers when she realized how hot the waffles still were.

Before she'd even managed to retrieve the syrup, a knock sounded on the front door.

Her gaze flew toward the entryway, and she stared, as if she'd never had someone knock on her door before. In truth, it wasn't often she had visitors. And certainly not in the past few days.

When another knock sounded, though, she felt she had no choice but to see who it was.

A quick glance out a side window told her what she should have already known. Jessie. That woman had a sixth sense that could rival a professional psychic any day of the week.

"Oh, good, you're up," Jessie said when Eliza opened the door.

Eliza gave a weak smile. "Don't pretend you didn't know. What tipped you off?"

"The get-well baskets. They've been sitting on your porch for two days. I went out for my morning walk, and BOOM, they were gone."

"But that was only ten minutes ago."

"Yes, I tend to have impeccable timing." Jessie peeked around Eliza, as if to see if she might have other visitors.

Eliza was already tired from standing and ushered the older woman in. "Who are you looking for?" She closed the door and didn't let Jessie's confused expression fool her. "Come on, out with it."

Jessie moved to a couch in the front room and made herself at home. "You misunderstand, dear. It's not that I was expecting anyone. I mean, maybe hoping that someone might be here, keeping you company. Helping out with whatever you need. People die from the flu, you know."

Eliza followed Jessie's lead and settled on the couch opposite her. "Yes, but rarely someone who takes care of their health the way I do. The flu doesn't have a chance against me."

"That's probably true." Jessie opened her mouth as if to say more but then stopped and shut it once again.

Eliza didn't want to be rude. It was nice of Jessie to drop by, but those waffles were calling her. She hadn't eaten since the day she'd decorated for the auction.

The auction.

She'd nearly forgotten that had even been a thing. The event had been days ago, and disappointment settled over her—she'd hated to miss it.

Between the auction, and now the movie screenings and tourists beginning to arrive, no wonder Jessie was coming by to see if Eliza was feeling better. She could probably use all the help she could get.

But Eliza was in no shape to run around town. Maybe the following day, after she'd gotten something to eat.

"I hope you don't think I'm a terrible host, but would you mind if I eat while we talk?" Eliza asked, pushing herself up from the couch. "It's been days since I've had something other than the water that I took my pain medication with."

Jessie's lips parted, and she leaped from the couch. "Of course. I'm so sorry. Let me help you."

And so Jessie ushered Eliza to a barstool at the counter, set the plate of waffles and a fork in front of her, then busied herself opening cupboards.

"Syrup?" she asked Eliza over her shoulder.

"Fridge, second shelf in the door." It was nice having someone take care of her. Some folks thought of Jessie as intrusive, always making others' business her own. But that was what made her special. She cared for everyone as if they were her own flesh and blood, and the town was better off for it.

Her breakfast ensemble complete, Eliza dug in. "I haven't had the chance to ask how the auction went," she said around a mouthful of waffle. Gosh, they were good. Some of the syrup escaped, and Eliza could feel it dripping down her lips, but the napkins were just out of reach. With a quick flick of her tongue, she managed to catch the drips.

"Oh, it was lovely. Everyone had a real nice time." Jessie busied herself wiping down counters that Eliza hadn't thought were dirty. Maybe Jessie was the type of person who always had to have something to do. "We managed to raise thirty thousand dollars."

"That's amazing," Eliza exclaimed, accidentally spraying waffle and syrup onto the counter. Now Jessie really did have something she could clean. Eliza hadn't thought the town would be able to raise anywhere near that on its own. Starlight Ridge, along with being a close-knit community, was also a prideful one. Not necessarily in a bad way, but they took pride in their town, and that pride was the reason this was their first ever fundraising event. Everyone in town loved offering a helping hand, but they'd rather suffer on their own than ask someone else for that same help.

"A fantastic start, for sure," Jessie said, wiping the counter where Eliza's food had landed. "And we'll raise much more from the movie screenings than first expected. I've raised prices three times on tickets, and the orders just keep coming in. The town council suggested adding extra screenings Friday night, and Elli had the idea that we could also place a donation box out in the theater's lobby. Of course, they might not want to donate more than they already have, but you never know. Doesn't hurt to ask."

Another knock on the door stole Eliza's attention. What was with everyone showing up this morning? Had *everyone* been watching for the get-well baskets to disappear? She moved to stand, but Jessie motioned for her to stay sitting.

"I can answer it. No need to tear you away from your breakfast. Probably just another get-well basket." She paused. "But maybe running a brush through your hair wouldn't be a terrible idea." And then she left to answer the door.

It couldn't be that bad, could it? Eliza tried to think back to the last time she'd looked in a mirror. Not since she'd gotten sick. Hadn't taken a shower. Might have brushed her teeth. Certainly hadn't changed her clothes.

Well, she hadn't changed her clothes if that first night didn't count, when she'd woken in bed to find that she still wore jeans and she'd wanted nothing more than to tear them off and slip into the most comfortable pair of pajamas she could find. It turned out that at three o'clock in the morning, while having the flu, Eliza had deemed a slinky nightgown that barely covered her butt the right choice. Couldn't bother with pants, apparently. The nightgown had been a prank gift from her sister at an extended family Christmas party, and Eliza was pretty sure this had been the first time she'd ever worn it. Oversized flannel pajamas were more Eliza's style—something she could cuddle up in with popcorn in front of a movie.

Luckily Eliza was wearing her floor-length robe, so Jessie hadn't seen anything she shouldn't. Rather than worrying about her hair, Eliza shoved in another mouthful of waffle. Seriously, these things had never tasted so good. More syrup escaped her lips, and she managed to catch those drips with her tongue too.

Someone cleared their throat.

Eliza turned, and there stood Travis, eyes wide. It wasn't until Jessie walked in from the front room, nudged him, and gave him the stink eye that he regained his composure.

There was no easy way out of this situation, and Eliza was torn between finishing her waffle and hightailing it out of there, never to return.

She chose the waffle.

Whatever this was, Jessie could deal with the awkward silence and figure out how to get them all gracefully through the situation. As long as it ended with Eliza in bed with a full stomach and everyone else out of her house.

Because from this moment forward, house guests were not going to be a thing in her home.

Ever.

Jessie cleared her throat before managing, "Travis stopped by on his way to a job to see how you're doing. Isn't that nice?" She then took a step back. "I think I'll tidy up in the front room a bit." And she disappeared.

Eliza shot Travis a polite smile. "Thank you. Just another day or so, and I think I'll be as good as new." She turned back to her waffle, hoping he'd get the hint.

He didn't.

Travis stepped forward and laid something on the counter next to her. "I heard that others had brought by baskets and didn't want to be the new guy who thought he was too good for that kind of thing." His voice was soft. "I'm sorry, I should have called first."

As he turned to leave, Eliza picked up the small item. It was a dumbbell carved out of wood, a hole drilled in the top and a chain hanging from it.

"Did you make this necklace yourself?" she asked, turning.

He paused, then faced her. "I had some free time."

Liar. There was no way that man had had a moment to himself since arriving in Starlight Ridge.

"It's lovely."

And she meant it. It was the sweetest thing someone had ever done for her.

Travis gave her a quick smile. "I know I acted all weird when

I realized...well, that there was more to you than meets the eye—"

"You mean, because I'm stronger than you," Eliza interrupted. She immediately wanted to take the words back, knowing she was ruining the sweet gesture that Travis was trying to make. But she didn't want to skirt around the issue—Travis had been avoiding her because he couldn't move the same boxes that she could. Eliza had seen it before, and she'd see it again. It was an issue that guys couldn't get over. And it was a sore spot for her.

Travis nodded. "Yeah. Anyway, it's something you should be really proud of. That takes a lot of discipline. Thought you might like a reminder."

Eliza turned back to her waffle and shoved the last bite into her mouth so he wouldn't see the moisture that had suddenly pooled in her eyes. It probably had something to do with just getting over the flu, and nothing to do with him being the first man who had ever told her she should be proud of her accomplishments rather than putting her down for them.

When she glanced over her shoulder, he was gone.

Eliza released a long breath and spun her legs around the barstool so she sat facing away from the kitchen counter.

"Jessie," she called, wondering if she had left with Travis.

"I'll be right there," Jessie answered. And then some quiet murmuring, like she was talking to someone else in the front room. Maybe Travis hadn't left after all.

A moment later, the two of them walked back in, and Jessie's eyes widened, while Travis's gaze dropped to the floor.

Eliza glanced between the two. "What?" She held out her arms and looked down, wondering if she'd spilled food all over herself without realizing it.

No, food wasn't the problem. In fact, Eliza kind of wished it had been.

Her robe had opened when she'd swung around on the seat, and she was now showing off her tiny nightgown that was apparently even tinier when she was sitting. "Oh, for goodness sake." Eliza leaped off the stool, retied her robe, and hurried upstairs, taking the steps two at a time. When passing the bathroom, she made the mistake of glancing inside and caught her reflection in the mirror.

She released a small gasp and stopped so fast, she nearly tripped. Entering the bathroom, Eliza stood in front of the mirror, horrified, and touched her hair. The normally silky-smooth hair that she couldn't ever get to do anything was now so matted that it looked like someone had made papier mâché with it. It stuck to her head at odd angles, and for a brief, terrifying moment, she wondered if the only way she'd be able to undo what it had become would be to shave it all off.

But her awful appearance didn't stop there. Eliza's face was pale, dark bags hung under her eyes, and syrup had somehow managed to escape cleanup and still resided on her chin. She looked like something out of a horror movie.

"I can't believe Jessie let me walk around like this." Eliza placed her hands on the counter in front of her, steadying herself. She closed her eyes. There were worse things.

Right?

Eliza was having trouble imagining anything worse than this.

What must Travis think?

He should have run from the house, screaming. But he hadn't batted an eye, instead presenting her with that beautiful gift.

Until she had flashed him, of course. Then his gaze had landed anywhere that Eliza wasn't.

Good thing she wasn't trying to impress Travis—unlike the rest of the town, who couldn't seem to let the poor man be.

She sucked in one last long breath, wiped the moisture from her eyes, and slipped down the hallway to her bedroom.

Jessie and Travis could let themselves out.

Because looking either of them in the eye was not something she'd be able to do for a very long time.

## 13

S tupid.

That was what it had been. Making that necklace for Eliza as a get-well gift. Who gives someone a wooden dumbbell as a present?

Travis hammered a baseboard in place at the bed and breakfast. A little boy—a guest—had apparently thought it fun to pry off all the baseboards in the room. Leanne and Isaac hadn't kicked the family out but had instead moved them to another room with a promise from the family that it wouldn't happen again. With the kickoff to summer the next day, the rooms were filling up fast, and this had been a bit of a maintenance emergency.

He pounded another nail, but with too much force, his frustration getting the best of him.

Travis hadn't heard from Eliza since his visit to her house, which said something about what she'd thought of it.

He'd also hoped the necklace would help soften the blow of what Jessie had done—what she had confided in him.

That Jessie was bestowing her "date" with Travis onto Eliza.

Relief had been Travis's first instinct.

Relief that it wasn't Jessie.

Relief that it wasn't Brenda.

Both very nice women, to be sure, but just not for him—not in that kind of way, anyway.

And Eliza?

Well, Travis had no interest in dating at all, but at least with her, he thought they might have some fun.

He wiped sweat off his brow. One baseboard down, three to go. The kid had been ruthless, and Travis doubted any room in the bed and breakfast would be safe from the boy's antics.

A knock on the door. "Housekeeping."

Before Travis could answer, Eliza bustled in with a cart filled with new sheets, towels, and travel-size soaps.

He stood so quickly, his head swam, and Eliza released a small scream.

They both stared for a moment before both started talking.

"I'm sorry, I—"

"Leanne told me that—"

They each stopped and released a small laugh.

Travis took a step forward. "Do you need me to leave? I'm fixing some baseboards that had the misfortune of meeting a very audacious boy, but I can come back."

Eliza gave a shake of her head. "No, that's fine. I won't be long. I should wait to vacuum until you're done anyway."

Travis stared for a moment too long before dropping his gaze to the hammer he still held. Eliza looked beautiful today, her hair up in its signature ponytail.

Funnily enough, he'd thought the same thing when she had been sick, with her hair all matted to one side. It had been sweet and made him want to stick around—help her feel better.

A different kind of beautiful.

*Where had that come from?* Travis thought with a start.

It should go back where it came from, wherever that was.

Because those were ideas that Travis couldn't—and shouldn't—be entertaining.

Not with Eliza. Not with anyone.

Not in the condition Travis was currently in.

And suddenly he worried about this date he was supposed to have with Eliza. The date that she didn't even know about. Maybe Jessie would forget about it and they'd never end up having it.

Jessie forget that she'd set up a date? Not likely.

"You okay?" Eliza asked, shaking him from his thoughts.

Travis realized that Eliza wasn't standing in front of him anymore but was now across the room, pulling sheets off the bed.

And he was there, still staring at the floor, like one of those creepy wax figures you see in a museum.

Travis spun back toward the baseboards. "Yeah. Just tired. You were right. Tourist season doesn't even officially kick off until this weekend, but I've certainly been busy."

"I guess you're probably not going to any of the movie screenings, then?" Eliza asked.

"Are you?" he asked, without really answering the question.

She released what sounded like a wistful sigh. "I wish. I thought I'd be running the movie from up in the booth—it's an old theater, and I've done it before—but the job went to someone else. I guess they're keeping it all hush hush because loads of people in town wanted to do it."

"Oh, yeah?" Travis tried not to sound too interested, but the truth was that the town council had asked him to do it. He'd just thought of it as another random job that they wanted him to do —which wasn't at all hardware related and had kind of annoyed him at the time, despite them offering to pay. But who wanted to be alone in a booth all weekend watching the same movie over and over? He'd rather be useful. Rather be fixing things.

Now he wondered why he was the chosen one, when so many others had wanted the opportunity. Maybe Eliza was right about the town's opinion of him.

Travis needed to set the record straight, because he was not as wonderful as they were making him out to be, and he certainly didn't deserve any special treatment.

"You know, it's funny," Eliza said as she worked on the corner of a fitted sheet. Every time she pulled it down, though, the opposite side popped off. She threw it a scowl, then turned pleading eyes toward Travis. She nodded toward the corner that was having trouble. "Do you mind?"

Travis walked over and pulled it taut. "What's funny?"

"Running movies from the booth isn't anyone's full-time job, we just kind of rotate, because the theater is only open a couple of weekends each month. But I usually do it because no one else wants to." They finished the four corners, and she shot him a quick smile. "Thanks."

He nodded and returned to his baseboards.

"I love it up there, though, sitting above everyone else in the theater. It's almost like I have a view from Heaven, looking down on everything that's happening. The boy who spills his popcorn because he was trying to keep it away from his sister. The girl who is trying to get up the guts to hold her date's hand but keeps chickening out at the last minute." She paused. "Oh, gosh, that made me sound like I'm pretending to be God or something, didn't it?" Eliza covered her face and released a laugh. "I just... I don't mind being alone. And there is something special about being alone in that box."

Travis understood how that might feel. "That sounds very similar to how I felt in Thailand. I wasn't alone, per say, but there was just a small group of us living in the middle of nowhere. And many times, I would be alone on a roof, and looking down and being able to see all of the other huts splayed out in front of me interspersed with the jungle...it was magical."

That was when Travis knew what he and Eliza would be doing on their date. But how to break it to her that they were going on one... Was it obligatory? What if she said no?

All his insecurities came flooding back. The ones that told him he wasn't good enough. That there was some sort of "it" factor that he didn't have. Travis knew he wasn't bad looking, and he was certainly strong and capable of holding his own—although that had been challenged as of late—but there was something Davis had that Travis didn't. And he couldn't, for the life of him, figure out what that was.

"Penny for your thoughts," Eliza said, watching him as she replaced pillowcases. She placed them at the head of the bed and then got to working on straightening the blanket. "You look very contemplative over there. And worried."

Was he really so transparent?

Maybe that had been the turn-off for Chloe. That she could always tell what he was thinking without him having to say it. And she didn't like where those thoughts were leading.

"Jessie bought me at the auction," he blurted out.

Wow, there were so many ways that had come out wrong, Travis didn't even know how to address them all.

Eliza raised an eyebrow before laughing. "Really. Tell me more."

This hadn't been the way he'd wanted the news broken—it should have been Jessie. Why hadn't she told Eliza?

"Jessie was going to tell you," he said. "That day I stopped by. You know the one where...you weren't quite feeling well yet."

Eliza stopped him before he could keep blabbering on. "Yes, I know the day. The one where I apparently looked like a sea monster, accidentally flashed everyone, and wanted to curl up in a corner and die." She was no longer looking amused.

"Uh...what?" Where had that come from?

His confusion must have been obvious—like every other emotion, apparently—because Eliza's frown had morphed into something else. Curiosity?

"You looked beautiful." When she snorted and turned away, he insisted, "You really did. You were real, you know. Genuine. And beautiful. And for the record, I didn't see anything when, you know..."

He stopped there. But he really hadn't seen anything. Just a woman who was a walking oxymoron. One who wore a floor-length robe that had flowers on it—much like something his grandmother would wear—but secretly wore sexy pajamas underneath. Travis didn't know which was the real her—or if it was both—but that intrigued him.

Eliza waved a hand through the air like she didn't believe him but wanted him to continue. "Okay, so you weren't as trau-matized that day as I was, good to know. But let's get back to the real issue at hand." She pulled a bottle of cleaner and a rag from the cart in front of her and walked toward the bathroom. "You're saying that Jessie came by to tell me that she bought you at the auction?" She released a laugh that said she thought the idea was completely ridiculous.

Which it was, for the record.

Even if the rest of this backwards town didn't think so.

"I don't know if that was her original intention for stopping by," Travis called to her from where he was fitting another base-board. "She hadn't known I was going to also stop by your place."

When Travis paused to hammer in a nail, Eliza called, "Continue."

He sucked in a long breath. "I was on the docket to give a donation at the auction. I knew that much. I was planning on donating a few hours of handyman work, and I told Jessie I'd rather donate a service than actual hardware. She agreed and put me down. I saw her write *service*."

Eliza popped her head back out. "But she didn't specify what kind of service, right?"

Travis nodded.

"Classic Jessie." Eliza disappeared for a brief moment, then reemerged with an armful of towels. "So what, instead of five hours of handyman work, she put you down for ten or something and then bought it herself? Caleb and Bree won my service, and they plan on using all five hours for babysitting. They just had a kid, you know. It definitely could have been worse."

Travis cleared his throat. "Uh...no. Not handyman work."

Eliza threw the dirty towels in a basket on the cart and leaned on it. "What did that woman do?"

"She may or may not have pranced me around stage and had single women bid on the opportunity to have a date with me." Just saying it made Travis's cheeks heat up. It had been embarrassing then, but it felt even more embarrassing talking about it after the fact.

Eliza's jaw dropped. "She didn't."

"She did. Told me afterwards that she was just trying the keep the mood light, and she knew it would probably bring in a lot of money for the library. I'm not sure I believe that was all there was to it, though."

"She means well," Eliza said, sinking onto the bed. "Truly, she does. Jessie never married, and I think she just wants to help us young, single things have a chance at love. But for her to do it in this way...well, it's wrong on so many levels."

Travis set his hammer down next to a stray baseboard and walked over to the bed, sitting next to Eliza. "I completely agree there."

"Wait." Eliza's gaze flew to Travis. "You said that Jessie

bought you in the auction. Do you mean to tell me she set that up so she could go on a date with you?" Her hand flew to her mouth, as if she couldn't imagine the horror. "That little cougar!"

It was time. He would tell her the truth and let the chips fall where they may. Travis knew that Eliza didn't think much of him, and he really didn't think this was going to go well. But then he saw the dumbbell.

Eliza was wearing the necklace.

"She didn't win the date for herself. She won it for you."

## 14

E liza stared.

Jessie winning the bid for herself hadn't made sense.

But this? Winning it for Eliza? That was Jessie 101.

"I had told Jessie to bid on something for me. Told her I had two hundred bucks saved up for it," she said, shaking her head. Eliza knew better than to blindly trust that Jessie would bid on a new wetsuit from the scuba shop or something equally useful. This was Eliza's fault for giving the woman free rein.

"Oh, this cost more than the two hundred bucks you gave her."

Great. Did Jessie expect Eliza to pay her the extra it had cost to win the bid?

Eliza's heart did a dive, and she asked weakly, "How much did this date with you cost?" She held her breath as she awaited his answer.

Travis looked like he didn't want to give it. "Three hundred and forty dollars."

Eliza jumped to her feet. "Three hundred and—"

Oh, that woman was going to get it.

Eliza snatched her phone from her back pocket and immediately called Jessie. They were going to clear this up right then and there.

Travis looked like he didn't know if he should be there for this conversation, so he wandered back over to his baseboards, put some headphones on, and busied himself on the opposite side of the room.

Just to be safe, Eliza stepped out into the hall.

"Hello?" Jessie sounded so sweet and unassuming, you'd never know what really lay under the surface until it was too late. Even now, Eliza was still learning.

"I don't have three hundred and forty dollars to pay for a date that I didn't want to go on in the first place," Eliza said, skipping any pleasantries.

A pause.

"Is this Eliza?"

Really, she was going to play it that way?

"You know who this is, Jessie. And I told you two hundred dollars. I wanted a hat or an ice cream cake. Maybe a new snorkel."

A small chuckle. "I see that you've finally talked with Travis. I wondered how long that would take. Longer than it should have, really."

Eliza groaned. "Jes-sie..."

"You really can't blame me, dear. You weren't specific about what you wanted from the auction. And don't worry about the excess money. Consider it an early Christmas present."

"You mean the holiday that is still seven months away?"

"Fine. A late Christmas present."

Eliza paced the hallway and rubbed her eyebrows. "Is it one that is exchangeable?"

She felt bad even asking it. Jessie must have desperately

wanted this for Eliza if she was willing to pay one hundred and forty dollars of her own money for it. But still...dating and romance and all that...it wasn't something that had ever been in the cards for Eliza. She didn't have time for it.

Not only that, but the memory of what Craig had done... It still stung. Of course, that was nothing compared to what her mother had done to her father.

And that was the dealbreaker—she wouldn't allow herself to do the same thing to someone else.

A long pause from the other end of the line.

"I'm afraid not, dear. This one is for keeps."

Eliza was unsure if Jessie was referring to the date or Travis himself. But either way, she knew she had to go on the date. She would feel too guilty not to.

"Okay. And thanks for the Christmas present. I feel bad I didn't get you anything."

A laugh on the other end. "Just you going on this date is enough. I'm sorry I was so sneaky about it, on both your and Travis's ends. But I knew it wasn't anything you two would readily agree to."

"You're right about that. For the past three days, every time I've asked what you had won for me, you kept telling me you'd deliver it later this week."

"It wasn't a lie if you think about it the right way," Jessie said. "Oh, sorry, I need to go. The oven just beeped. But have fun on your date, and I expect to hear all about it afterward. Spare no detail."

"Not happening."

"Consider that your present for me."

And then Jessie hung up, off to rescue a batch of tarts, no doubt.

"Oh, that woman." Eliza slipped her phone into her pocket

and stepped back into the guest room to grab her cart. One room down, minus a good vacuuming, five more to go.

She threw a quick glance at Travis and saw he was sitting with his back against the wall, headphones still on, but from the look on his face, he had heard it all.

He looked like...he cared. Like even though he'd been tricked into this date, he'd actually wanted to go on it.

But that wasn't possible. The man had been shown off at an auction like cattle at the county fair.

And yet...

"Travis, look, it's not that—"

He held up a hand. "It's fine. Say no more. I know you didn't ask for this. How about if you don't go out with me and I'll tell Jessie you did. I'll say we didn't click, our personalities didn't mesh, but you're a lovely person and thank you for trying. No harm, no foul, and the library still gets its donation. Really, it's fine."

And then he picked up his tools and headed for the door, the baseboards not yet complete.

"Don't you need to—"

He didn't even turn around when he said, "I can finish up once you're done. Don't want to get in your way."

"Travis, stop." Eliza hurried in front of him, blocking his exit. "I am going to go on that date with you. But I'm nearly finished in here, so if someone needs to leave, I will, so you can focus on your work. I really am sorry you overheard that, though. My voice tends to rise ten decibels when I'm stressed." She blew out a frustrated breath. "It's just that Jessie can be so infuriating sometimes, and yet no one can ever stay mad at her. It's one of her finer qualities."

Travis gave a slow nod. "Okay. Guess I'm bought and paid for, so I don't have much choice in the matter." He turned and moved toward his supplies.

The way he said it...so sad...it made it that much more awful. "I'm not going to force you to do this. I'm not going to make you go out with me," Eliza said, the words tumbling out. "If you want to back out, then we can invent a story about our less-than-ideal date. If that's what you really want."

Travis glanced back at her, his expression conflicted. "Saturday night," he finally said. "I'll pick you up at six-thirty." And then he turned back to the job at hand.

Eliza rolled the housekeeping cart out of the room, but just around the corner. And then she slid down next to the wall like Travis had done just minutes before.

Why was everything so hard?

She never came up with an answer.

Saturday. Six-thirty.

Eliza looked out the window. He hadn't arrived yet.

Would Travis stand her up? She had no idea—she still didn't have his number.

Even as she thought it, Eliza knew she'd never use the number if she did have it. If he didn't care enough to remember their date, then she shouldn't care enough to call to remind him. It would give Eliza the out that she needed. In fact, she would be relieved if Travis stood her up. It would be a blessing.

And Eliza kept telling that lie to herself, ignoring the fact that she had changed her clothes three times and then repeatedly let her hair down, just to put it back up in a ponytail, and then let it down again.

Eliza looked at the clock. Six forty-five.

The man was late. That was it. He'd lost his chance.

She didn't even know if it had been a chance that he'd wanted, but regardless, he'd lost it.

Eliza glanced out the window one last time. Her breath

caught. Sometime after she'd last looked, Travis had shown up. But he was pacing in front of the house, like he was summoning the courage to knock on her door.

She bit back a smile. That was such a seventeen-year-old thing to do.

And it was adorable.

Eliza debated whether she should make things easier on him and let herself out but then decided against it. He'd know she'd been watching him pace, and she didn't want to start things out weird. Or weird*er*. They'd surpassed weird when they'd both been forced into this situation.

It took another minute, but eventually the knock came.

She counted to five under her breath before she approached the door and opened it.

Even after seeing Travis through the window, Eliza's heart stalled. He looked good—too good. His hair was gelled, and he wore a button-up dress shirt with a pair of nice slacks. She glanced down at her sundress, suddenly feeling underdressed.

"I'm sorry," Eliza said, taking a step back. "I didn't realize it was a fancy kind of date. I can go change—"

But then Travis smiled, his nervousness seemingly dissipated by Eliza's own. "You look perfect." And then he held out a hand.

Taken aback, Eliza took his hand and allowed him to lead her outside. She turned back to lock the front door and, as she did, slipped the elastic from her ponytail so that her hair fell onto her shoulders. She couldn't say exactly why she had done it, only that there was something about Travis that made her want to be at her best, and she didn't think her ponytail had made the cut.

They walked in silence, and Eliza searched for the right words. She didn't see a car, which meant wherever they were going was close enough to walk, and she was grateful she had worn her low-heel shoes.

"You look nice," she finally said, unable to think of anything else to say.

"As do you." Travis's words escaped quickly but died just as fast.

Okay, this was officially the most awkward date Eliza had ever been on.

They walked past the florist shop, where Natalie was just closing up, then Mueller Market, and then the old library.

"Did you ever visit the library as a child, or had it already closed down?" Travis asked.

Finally, a topic of conversation. Except, it was the last topic Eliza would have chosen. It was her fault for not coming up with something first.

She played with the strap of her purse, wondering how to answer. "I only remember bits and pieces of it. My mother would take me every afternoon, and she would read to me in a little story nook they had set up in a corner with bean bags and a picture of Peter Rabbit. Other children would come and read, but they would never take our corner, because they knew that was our special place."

"And then the storm came."

Eliza took a shuddered breath. "No, then my mom died."

Well, that was an excellent way to kill a date before it had started. Bring up your dead mother. But the guy had asked. That didn't change the fact that if conversation had been difficult before, it would now be impossible.

Or so Eliza had thought.

Instead, Travis turned kind eyes on her and simply said, "I'm sorry. That had to be so hard."

He didn't try to tell her things like *It was her time* or *She's in a better place.* All the things people said to try to help you feel better but unknowingly made it worse.

"Yeah, it was."

A pause as they turned left onto the boardwalk. They passed Starlight Chocolate Confections, where tourists were already taking pictures, as it had been one of the main filming locations for *Amaretto.* No one was giving the hardware store, the scuba shop, or the dry cleaners a second look. Not the tattoo parlor either. When they reached the end of the boardwalk, they paused in front of an Italian bistro that had recently opened.

"Would you be okay eating here?" Travis asked.

Eliza had been annoyed when the Italian place had first moved in on the boardwalk. It didn't fit the seaside theme the town was known for, and she'd avoided it, purposely going all the way out to the edge of town to the cafe for a pastrami sand-wich. That would show them.

But every time she did, the tantalizing aromas that escaped the bistro had slowly broken through her barriers, and she knew the time had come.

Eliza was going to go Italian.

"That actually sounds good."

Travis opened the door for her while giving his watch a quick glance. His brow furrowed before he shot an embarrassed smile her way. "I know I was late picking you up, but it turns out that I've seriously misjudged the time." A pause. "Would you be okay with getting our food to go?" His smile wavered, like he was worried what she'd think of the request.

It was true that Eliza was unsure what to make of getting food to go on a date, but this was his thing, so she'd go along with it.

"Of course. No problem."

She only hoped he didn't expect her to eat chicken parmesan

while walking the beach for a sunset stroll or something stupidly romantic like that. If so, Eliza knew her clumsy ways, and the chicken wouldn't get far without becoming fish bait.

As it turned out, it was a good thing they weren't eating in, because the restaurant was packed with no open tables. That didn't happen often—if ever—in Starlight Ridge. Must be thanks to Jessie's fundraising efforts.

Thankfully, Travis didn't expect her to eat while walking the beach, instead ushering Eliza around the corner and up the steps of the movie theater that had already drawn a large crowd.

"Oh, I don't think outside food is allowed in there," Eliza said, pausing on the bottom step. She could just imagine the aroma that would fill the theater if they tried bringing in their chicken parmesan and lasagna, not to mention the garlic bread. They'd be thrown out before opening credits.

Which brought her to the question, how had Travis managed to snag tickets to this anyway? They were like three hundred bucks a piece now.

Travis laughed and motioned for her to follow him, their to-go bag swinging from one finger. "Trust me."

And then he walked inside, expecting her to follow. All right. She would. But if they got kicked out, or she found out that he'd sneaked into the theater without tickets, then this first date was definitely going to be the last.

But wouldn't it be anyway? They were only there because Jessie had forced their hands.

Eliza followed Travis inside, but he didn't move toward the main theater. Instead, he swerved to the left toward a door that was nearly camouflaged against the wall.

The door that would lead them upstairs to the control booth.

"You don't mean to tell me..."

"That I'm the man they chose to run the movie this week-end? Yes. I'm sorry I didn't tell you earlier, but I was sworn to secrecy. And I'm sorry for the food to go, but I had to get here in time for the seven-thirty showing."

Dumbfounded that the town would trust something so important to Travis, a man who had barely been in town for a month, Eliza followed him through the door and up a set of dark stairs.

## 15

Travis hoped he hadn't made a mistake. He knew it was universally frowned on to take a woman to your place of employment for a date—especially at the exact time you were expected to work. And he was expecting her to eat her dinner out of a Styrofoam box. Not exactly something at the top of the list of how to win a woman's heart.

But when she entered the box that sat above the theater, and her lips twitched up into a smile, he took that as a good sign.

Three rolling office chairs sat in front of the electronics panel, and there was a side table where they could set their food. The chairs were the comfy kind with plenty of padding, and, considering how many hours he'd already been in the box that day, it was definitely needed.

"I've never been up here for an event like this," Eliza said, leaning forward and peering down on the growing audience.

She pointed at a man who had just walked in and was trying to find a seat with a woman who looked to be his wife. "What do you think his story is?"

The man wore a fedora and sunglasses, even though the

theater lights were dim, and his wife wore a tight sleeveless dress that barely covered what it needed to.

"Mafia," Travis immediately responded. "Has to lie low for a bit and thought that Starlight Ridge would be the perfect place to go unnoticed."

Eliza laughed. "He would be right. Crazy tourist gear will never stand out in Starlight Ridge, so kudos on him."

Travis glanced at his phone. "Time to roll." He moved to start the movie and lower the lights but paused and turned to Eliza. "Would you like to do the honors?"

Her lips parted in surprise. "Really?"

Travis lifted a shoulder, pleased that despite the unorthodox approach he'd risked taking, Eliza seemed to be enjoying herself. "I know you said you wished you'd been chosen to handle the booth this weekend, and I thought you might like it."

Eliza held up a finger. "Let me clarify. It was more like, 'Really? You brought me here so I could do your job while you sit back and take it easy?' I mean, really, how many dates have you been on, Travis?"

Oh.

Travis hadn't meant it that way.

But then Eliza grinned and rolled her chair up to the panel. She had been teasing him. "Just for future reference, just because it works on me doesn't mean you should do this with other women."

And then she started the film, the lights dimming.

Travis opened his food and watched the opening scene, enthralled, as the actor, Eli Hunt, came on the screen, nearly unrecognizable. He was dressed in leather for one thing—something Eli would never do—and was speaking in a British accent, stumbling around, drunk.

This was definitely a side of Eli that Travis would never have thought he'd see. He knew it was supposed to be a bit of a serious moment, but seeing Eli like this was almost comical.

"I think we should finally get a bar in Starlight Ridge and name it after Eli's character," Travis said with a smirk. He shoved a forkful of lasagna in his mouth.

Eliza laughed. "The town would never go for it. Every business that comes through has to be approved by the town council, and they'd rather see a chain restaurant set up shop than allow a bar here, and that's saying something."

"But there's a tattoo parlor," he pointed out. He thought that was much more risqué than a place that served drinks and had a few pool tables.

Eliza took her time cutting her chicken as she threw a little smile his way. "True. But when you have a bar, you also have the possibility of drunk tourists. Tattoos are something the individual person will regret, but the other? Starlight Ridge doesn't want to deal with that. You introduce alcohol, you introduce a whole lot of other problems."

Travis lifted a shoulder. He supposed she had a point. And it hadn't seemed to diminish the number of tourists at all. If they really wanted to drink, they could treat the town as BYOB— bring your own booze.

They settled into their chairs as they ate. Eliza propped her feet up on the table in front of her, happily eating through her chicken parmesan as they watched the movie.

"Can I ask you a question?" she finally asked.

"If I'm allowed the same in return."

She paused at that, apparently weighing the risk. She must have decided it was a safe bet, because she nodded.

"Why did you come here? I mean, I know that you came from Thailand to take over Davis's store. But why? Thailand couldn't have been all that bad, right?"

Oh, they were jumping to the big stuff. The heavy stuff.

"You have to be honest," she hurriedly said.

He really was too transparent.

It took him a minute to put his thoughts into words. "I didn't have anything left to stay for."

Eliza raised an eyebrow, urging him to continue.

He really didn't want to do this. At all. With anyone. But especially on a first date. Travis gave a resigned sigh. "I was in love with a woman. We ran the service organization together. I thought that eventually she would see me in the same way. But she didn't. Granted, for the first few years I was there, I wasn't exactly the type of guy you'd want to bring home to your mother. But for her, I could have been. By the end, I really was trying, but it wasn't enough."

Eliza chewed her food slowly. "So, you left the home you loved because of a girl."

When she put it that way, it sounded pathetic. Because yes, he had given everything up because of a girl. A woman. Chloe. But she had been so much more than that. She had been the reason for it all. And that was the most pathetic part.

"Yup. Maybe it was supposed to happen this way—maybe she was supposed to meet Davis. Because then I could at least move on with my life—try to figure out who I am without her."

Eliza held up a finger. "The same woman that Davis stayed for?" She gave a low whistle. "That must be some woman."

A corner of Travis's lips tilted up. "Yes, she is."

"And now your heart it closed off, and you are trying to find your place in this world."

Eliza said it so sincerely, and yet it came across as the most melodramatic thing he'd ever heard. Which made the truth of the statement that much more embarrassing.

"Something like that." Travis pulled in a shuddered breath. "Now I get to ask a question."

It was Eliza's turn to look worried, and she returned her attention to the movie in front of them.

"What is your favorite color?"

Eliza's gaze whipped to him. If she could bring out the heavy stuff, so could he. Her lips quirked up at the edges. "Green."

He nodded and pretended to write it down. "Very interesting. That explains a lot."

She turned so she fully faced him. "And what exactly would that be?"

Travis had no idea, so he just smiled. "Can't go revealing all my secrets."

"Okay. I see how you're going to play this." Eliza smiled, then shoved another bite of chicken into her mouth. "But just so you know," she said around the food, "no secret is safe here in Starlight Ridge."

Which brought up the real question Travis wanted to ask. Every day he saw her out running the beach first thing in the morning, and again as the sun began to set. She was the captain of the town's volleyball team and had done competitive weightlifting. Apparently, before that, it had been surfing.

"You're always moving, always going," he said. "Never settling on one thing. Why?"

Eliza paused, a forkful of food halfway to her mouth.

There was probably a better way to phrase the question, but he really wanted to know. Her jobs in town were endless, whatever someone needed. She wasn't passionate about any one sport, changing constantly. She lived alone, so she obviously hadn't settled on one man.

Eliza turned back to the movie.

Maybe he'd crossed a line.

"I was wrong," she finally said, her voice quiet. "There are some secrets that are safe in Starlight Ridge."

And then she was quiet, and Travis didn't push.

He bet there were a lot of secrets in Starlight Ridge, and he realized he'd need to become better at hiding his.

## 16

E liza stared ahead at the screen. The evening had been perfect. She couldn't have planned a better date herself. The food, the movie from the box...the company. And then she'd had to go and ruin it by getting all deep with a guy she didn't even know.

All he'd asked was that she reciprocate. If she'd wanted him to go deep, she'd been expected to go deep as well.

But when push came to shove, she couldn't do it. She'd frozen.

And then the rest of the night had been filled with scattered, awkward chitchat, with most of their attention directed at the movie.

It had been so romantic, sitting up there in the dim light, above everyone else in the theater.

Eliza had to admit that she'd even been tempted to kiss him once or twice. The garlic bread helped put an end to those thoughts. But so had she.

Why did she always self-sabotage like that? So what, she had a past. The guy already knew her mom had died. It wouldn't be a stretch to tell the rest of the story.

But she'd clammed up.

Maybe because she'd only told the story to one other person, and he had treated her like she was crazy. It hadn't been the main reason Craig had left her, but she was sure it had contributed.

Craig had told her she couldn't outrun death.

Logically, Eliza knew that was true.

But she was always left with the nagging thought, what if she could?

The end credits rolled, and Eliza stood, looking for the garbage can.

"Did you want to stay for the Q&A?" Travis asked, bringing the lights back up in the theater.

With no garbage can in sight, Eliza sat back down. She didn't answer right away, conflicted between wanting to stay but also wanting to put an end to the awkwardness.

"I won't be offended if you want to head home early," he assured her, though he did look disappointed.

Why did he have to be so kind when it was her fault the date had turned awkward?

He gave her a small, sad smile and stood as if to leave. Eliza probably should have agreed to cut the night short but surprised herself by instead grabbing Travis's hand, preventing him from walking away. His gaze snapped to her, and she dropped his hand. She couldn't forget the feel of it, though—the calluses, the strength.

"Let's stay," she said.

He gave a hesitant nod and then sat back down, his gaze wary.

"You know my mom died," she started, unsure why she was telling this to a man who was practically a stranger. But she felt like she could trust him—should trust him. And this was something that had weighed heavily on her heart for a very long time.

Travis gave another nod, as if afraid if he said anything, she'd change her mind and stop talking.

Here went nothing.

"She had a heart attack. Heart disease runs in my family—it's genetic. And it's always waiting just around the corner. My mom did everything right, mostly because her dad hadn't, and he'd died young. But it wasn't enough. She was taken from my family when I was six years old."

Below them, Eli walked in front of the theater crowd, Leanne with him. But Travis's attention wasn't on the famous actor. His gaze was on Eliza, and her alone. Even though he didn't say anything, it gave her the courage to continue.

"About ten years ago, I went in for a routine checkup, and Patty told me my cholesterol was high. High enough that if it got any worse, she was going to place me on medication to control it. Medication that is usually associated with old people. Not someone in their twenties."

Travis finally spoke. "I know of it."

"Then you know of its side effects. The headaches and muscle soreness. The memory issues. And how a lot of people choose not to take it because they'd rather deal with the threat of dying than live like that."

Travis reached out to give her hand a squeeze. It wasn't a romantic touch but the touch of someone who understood. "My grandfather. He ended up dying only a few months after stopping the medication."

So, Travis really did know. But once again, it had been an older person. She shouldn't be dealing with something like this at her age. It made her angry every time she thought about it.

"I went to the city to get my labs rechecked—make sure Patty hadn't made a mistake. At first, the doctors dismissed me. I was young. I wasn't overweight. But when I told them about my family history, they were forced to look at it differently. And then they told me the same thing Patty had. It was genetic. Nothing I could do about it. If my cholesterol went any higher, I'd need the medication." Her voice warbled, and she paused to rein in her emotions. "My mom was on the medication. She had all the side effects, and it still didn't do her any good."

Travis remained quiet but scooted his chair closer to hers. Eliza could tell that he had questions, but he didn't ask them. Just sat next to her, holding her hand, being there for her. The complete opposite of when she'd told Craig. Maybe Jessie was right—maybe this one was different.

"Anyway, I decided I was going to prove them wrong. The city doctor told me there was nothing I could do to lower my cholesterol—that it wasn't a matter of *if* I would need to take the medication but *when*. So I went on the internet to find out what normal people did to lower theirs. It was all the usual stuff. Exercise. Healthy eating. Less saturated fats. More good fats. Stop smoking, which I didn't do anyway. And so I took it to the extreme. And I've been trying to outrun my destiny ever since."

Eliza released a long breath. "And that is why I change sports every couple of years—because I get bored of them. Believe it or not, sports are not something I'm passionate about. But between exercising and eating a mostly clean diet, with a few of Adeline's chocolates on cheat days, I've been able to keep my cholesterol down. If I pause, though—if I slack off—it comes right back up again. So I keep going."

Travis seemed to be holding her hand tighter now, as if that would help it all go away. "That has to be so difficult—like running a lifelong marathon. Never feeling like you can stop."

That was exactly it. How was Travis so understanding—how did he just...get it?

"Exactly."

"Can I ask one thing, though, without getting into trouble?"

Okay, so maybe not as understanding as Eliza had thought.

But she was curious, so she nodded, giving him the go-ahead.

"I understand what you are running from. But what are you running to?"

Eliza didn't understand the question. There was no destination—no finish line. She was literally just running. To live.

Travis tried again, phrasing it slightly differently this time. "What does it matter if you live until you're thirty-five or ninety-five, if there is no one, or nothing, you are living for? I mean, I know you have this town, and you have friends. But surely you hadn't planned on living alone, doing odd jobs around town, and playing sports that you don't even like for your entire life. You're so busy running that you're missing out on all the things that make you happy." He paused. "I guess that's my real question. What makes you happy?"

Eliza stole her hand back from his. So much for understanding. Travis was the same as the rest of them, always telling her that she was doing it wrong. That she was missing out.

"You act like you know me, like I couldn't possibly be happy under the circumstances." She stood so fast that her chair rolled into the wall behind her. "I should have seen that you're like Craig. Maybe a little kinder in the way you say things, but underneath it all, you're no different."

Travis's brows scrunched in confusion. "Craig?"

"Yeah, my ex-fiancé. See, I did try having all the things that make me happy. But it had been at a time when I was competing in weightlifting, and Craig didn't like that too much. Said I was taking this cholesterol thing too far—too seriously. But it wasn't until his brother goaded Craig and me into an arm-wrestling competition—and I won—that he left me. Apparently, he didn't like that his fiancée was stronger than him."

A flicker of guilt passed over Travis's face, no doubt in memory of the box-moving incident.

"You're all the same," she said. When Travis stood, she shook her head. "No need. I'll walk myself home."

And then she left.

And Travis didn't follow.

## 17

Travis stayed until the end of the Q&A session, going over in his mind what he could have done differently—what he could have said differently. But when it came down to it, he had said exactly what he'd meant. He hadn't meant that Eliza should quit exercising or trying to be healthy.

But she was so fixated on that one thing, fear was ruling everything she did. Travis had no idea what goals she'd had in life before that fateful day a decade earlier, but he could bet that it didn't involve doing just enough to survive. Eliza was smart and driven—she needed purpose.

Travis could say all this because he knew what that was like. He'd never looked beyond the service organization for the six years he was there, because staying meant being with Chloe. Even if it wasn't in the exact way he'd been hoping, staying had meant that he never had to lose her.

And sure, he loved the Thai people and he loved helping others, and it had broken his heart to leave.

But when it came down to it, whether he liked it or not, every decision he'd made over those six years had been because of Chloe.

That was when it dawned on him. This was what he needed to say to Eliza. Because she thought he was talking from a place of judgment, and he wasn't. Far from it.

Travis shut down the booth, locked the door, and hurried from the theater. He glanced at his phone. Eleven. Was that too late to drop by Eliza's place? Maybe. But he still didn't have her phone number, and he wasn't going to let her avoid him again.

Eliza had infiltrated his life, and Travis found himself looking forward to each day, hoping he'd see her. Whether it was a brief glimpse as she ran along the beach, or like when they'd ended up working in the same room at the bed and breakfast.

Travis speed-walked toward Eliza's house.

She was going to think he was a stalker, knocking on her door so late. Not leaving her alone, when she obviously didn't want to be around him. From day one, he'd managed to offend her. He could admit that some of those times had been entirely his fault. Like the first day they'd met. But not all of them.

When Travis reached her house, he hesitated, his fist raised to knock, but not sure if he could do it.

Bur really, what did he have to lose?

He knocked.

And held his breath.

Should he knock again, or just leave and try again another day?

When Eliza didn't answer, Travis decided to leave it. Even if she was awake and knew he was there, he shouldn't push it. Shouldn't try to make her give him a chance and listen to what he had to say.

But just as he'd turned to walk away, the lock on the front door clicked and the door swung open.

Eliza hadn't changed out of the sundress she'd been wearing earlier, but her eyes were moist like she'd been crying.

Had he caused that?

"I'm sorry if I said something that hurt you—that wasn't my intention," he said, shuffling his feet. They wanted to run, but he forced them to stay put. "I've been where you are, I spoke from experience, but it didn't come across in the way I'd meant. And for that I'm sorry." And that was it. That was all he'd come to say.

Travis turned and started to walk away, his footsteps heavy. He hadn't expected anything in return, but then he heard Eliza calling his name, hurrying after him.

When she reached him, he saw she was fingering the necklace he had given her.

"I'm strong because I need to be, but you were right," she said, the words coming out fast. "I've been hiding behind that strength. Pretending. I'm not living the life I want. I want to be a physical therapist and open up a practice right here in Starlight Ridge. If anyone gets injured, they have to make lengthy trips to the city to see a specialist. I don't want them to have to do that. And I want a family. And friends who aren't afraid that I'm going to pressure them into being on a competitive volleyball team that they don't really want to be on. And I want to kiss you."

And she did.

Without any warning, Eliza leaned in and pressed her lips against Travis's. The kiss was soft and warm, and before Travis could wrap his head around what was happening, she'd pulled away, seeming shocked but pleased with what had just happened. It was almost like the kiss was a declaration of some kind—telling the world that she was going to do what she wanted and not live in fear anymore.

And then Eliza, fingering the necklace once more, said, "Thank you." And she ran inside her house and shut the door, the lock clicking back in place.

Travis stared at the front door for a long time before he remembered he still needed to walk home.

Seemed they were on good terms again. Weird terms, but good.

TRAVIS WOKE to the sound of reggae music from the chocolate shop next door. His neighbor Adeline seemed to have some weird ritual where she blasted the same music at seven each morning as she made her truffles for the day. At least he had no need for an alarm clock. And it could be worse. If it were teen pop music or country, he would be far less forgiving.

Even though Travis was wide awake now, he didn't get out of bed, instead staring at the ceiling.

He could not stop thinking about that kiss. Eliza's lips on his. How close she had been, and how he was kicking himself for not returning it. For not taking her into his arms and showing her how much that kiss meant to him.

And then Chloe's face popped up, dashing the image, and guilt replaced any happiness he'd dared have.

He had loved Chloe for six years, and within just a few weeks after leaving, suddenly he was having feelings for someone else?

Travis knew it wasn't logical to feel guilty over a woman who clearly didn't return his feelings. But he wasn't supposed to get over heartbreak quite that easily. And if this was some kind of a rebound thing, he didn't want to get Eliza mixed up in that.

She deserved better.

If it was a rebound thing, though, why couldn't he stop thinking about her?

It was when Jessie walked into his hardware store later that day that he thought of a way to discover the answer.

Jessie was handing out flyers, of course—it seemed that passing out flyers was nearly a full-time job for the woman—and she asked him if he could hang one in his window. "The results are in from last weekend," she told him, "and we are having a special town council to discuss what this means in regards to moving forward with the library."

She wouldn't give him further details but merely winked and smiled. In other words, it had been a smashing success.

"And thank you so much for stepping in at the last minute to run the movie booth," Jessie said, opening the door to leave. "It saved me the headache from hearing everyone fighting over it. Honestly, you'd think they were children the way they were arguing over whose turn it was."

"Why don't you hire someone part time?" Travis asked. "Then no one could get mad over it."

"We only show movies a couple of times a month," Jessie said. "And for special occasions. It's just not a full-time kind of job, you know? Eliza, actually, is the one we usually hire, but in this situation...well, everyone wanted to be a part of such a big event, so we thought it better to go outside the usual crowd."

Jessie stood in the doorway, not coming but also not going. Instead, she watched him with a mischievous glint in her eye. "Speaking of Eliza..."

And here it was.

It has been four days since their date at the movie screening, and Travis was surprised it had taken the matchmaker this long to make her appearance.

Travis returned her smile and leaned against the checkout counter. "We went out on Saturday night. She actually helped me in the booth at the screening, so she still got her wish of running the show."

Jessie tsked. "You brought her to work as a date? No wonder there hasn't been a second one."

Even if it had gone well, they hadn't had time to go out on another date. What did Jessie expect from people nowadays?

"I think it probably has more to do with the fact that she doesn't like me much." It hurt for Travis to admit as much, but even considering the kiss at the end of the evening, Travis was everything Eliza wasn't looking for. She liked being alone. Or maybe she just thought she did, until the right guy would come along and sweep her off her feet.

He'd seen it before, and he was sure he would see it again.

But it wouldn't be Travis.

He was always the friend—the confidant that women felt like they could trust and share their feelings with.

But not the one they brought home. Not the one they introduced to their parents.

"Nonsense," Jessie said with a laugh. "There is no way that woman, or any woman for that matter, wouldn't be interested in you. You just have to give her a chance—come around more often. She'll be at the town meeting tomorrow; you could always save her a seat."

Travis rubbed the back of his neck. "I don't know..."

Jessie waved one of the flyers in the air. "Seven o'clock. Don't be late."

And then she hurried down the boardwalk, handing out flyers to anyone who wasn't a tourist.

It wouldn't hurt to stop by, see how the fundraising efforts went.

A flutter in Travis's chest told him that even the possibility of seeing Eliza again made him nervous. And that maybe he liked her more than he wanted to admit. And that if this was a rebound thing, he wanted more of it.

Travis sighed and buried his head in his hands. He wasn't ready for life outside Thailand.

Life outside Chloe.

## 18

"All right, all right, quiet down." Erwin sat in front of the crowd, Patty and Jessie to his left, and Bree and Caleb to his right, their newborn sleeping in a baby carrier on the floor next to Bree's feet.

Eliza had walked in late, and she scanned the crowd, finally spotting an empty chair near the back. She slipped in, and Erwin began reading the minutes from the last meeting.

"Hello again."

Eliza nearly fell off her chair when she realized she'd plunked herself down next to Travis Matkin. The first date she'd had in a long time. Her first date that had been bought at an auction ever. And the first time she'd kissed a man in years. Three years, to be exact.

And there wasn't going to be a second time for anything on that list.

There couldn't be.

Though she was having a difficult time coming up with reasons why. She'd had plenty of good excuses just a month ago when Travis had first come to town, but now she couldn't for the life of her think what any of them were.

She'd come up with a list later, after the meeting.

Eliza gave him a polite smile, as if they hadn't bared their souls to each other in the theater booth. As if he hadn't given her the handmade necklace she wore every day, reminding her of her strength. Reminding her that she didn't need to be ashamed of who she was.

"Hello."

A pause.

"Lovely evening for a town meeting," he said.

This time her smile was genuine as she fought a laugh. "Yes, quite."

"Tourists keeping you busy?"

"Very."

Erwin paused mid-sentence, glancing up from his paper. "Whoever's chattering back there, if I'm boring you, you're quite welcome to leave and come back when you've decided you'd like to hear what I have to say."

Eliza covered her mouth, trying to trap her laughter, and saw that Travis's lips were tightly sealed, as if he were doing the same.

Erwin cleared his throat. "Very well, I'll continue." And he did. For a very long time. Things about litter cleanup and whose job it was to pick up the dog poop that kept mysteriously showing up along the beach. Eliza was pretty sure it was Erwin's dog who was doing it. He'd hired a teenager to walk the dog when he couldn't get away from his restaurant, and Eliza knew for a fact that the teenager paid more attention to his phone than to what the dog was doing.

She considered saying something, because that would be a sure-fire way to get things exciting. Erwin would be intensely offended that she would suggest that the dog poop problem was in fact his problem. And then accusations would start flying about "kids these days," and someone would suggest there be an age requirement for cell phones in town. According to some residents, cell phones were the root of everything that was wrong with young people. Because "back in my day, I didn't have a phone. I had to work hard and find other ways to entertain myself."

But as entertaining as that all would have been, Eliza was more interested in the fate of the library they had worked so hard to raise funds for. Because as much as her memories of the library brought tears, they also brought joy. And she wanted the other children in town to know what that joy felt like. The joy of searching through books you've never seen before, of being allowed to take them home. Reading in the hidden library corners with your mother, or on your own. The things you could discover there.

Every child deserved that.

And so, Eliza stayed quiet.

At long last, they got to the main discussion topic of the evening.

Erwin stood still for a moment, as if frozen in time, staring at the sheet of paper in front of him. "I am pleased to tell you that the movie screenings over the weekend raised two hundred and twenty thousand dollars." There was a collective gasp and excited whispers throughout the room. "Combined with the thirty thousand we were able to raise from the auction, that brings us to two hundred and fifty thousand."

More excited whispers.

That was because those gathered didn't know how much money it took to rebuild a library. Eliza's heart sank, and she turned to Travis. "It isn't enough, is it?"

Travis shook his head, his lips pulled into a frown.

"What if we put away that money and held another movie screening next year? Maybe it would become an annual thing. That could work, right?"

Travis hesitated. "It could. But I don't know if holding the same event with the same movie two years in a row would have the same pull."

He must have seen the disappointment in Eliza's features, because he quickly added, "But what do I know? I'm just the handyman."

Just the handyman. Right.

Travis was just the handyman like Eliza was just the odds-and-ends girl. Each of them a jack of all trades, master of nothing.

"Hey, do you want to get out of here?" Eliza surprised herself by asking. But the room was getting stuffy, the walls starting to close in. She needed space.

Travis's eyebrows rose in surprise, but he nodded and followed her out of the community center. The warm evening air enveloped them, and she breathed in deeply.

Travis held back, as if he was unsure how close she wanted him. She could imagine why, considering how she'd left things the last time they'd seen each other. Like she was a crazy person, mad at him one moment, and kissing him the next.

Oh, that kiss.

Travis shoved his hands into his pockets. "You feeling okay?"

"Yeah, fine. Maybe a little lightheaded, but really, I just needed to get out of there."

He gave a slow nod, like he didn't know what she expected of him, his gaze flitting back to the community center as though he thought he should go back.

Eliza traced an imaginary shape on the ground with her foot as she searched for something to say—something that could dispel the awkwardness of inviting Travis outside but not knowing what to do now that they were there.

"Do you ever feel like you're holding yourself back?" she

asked. "Like if you were a different person, you could have accomplished so much more—been someone truly great?"

Shoot, why did she always go for the deep stuff? She still didn't know Travis's favorite color, even though he now knew hers. And yet she had to jump into all this crazy philosophical stuff.

Travis motioned with his head for her to follow him, and they walked down the sidewalk toward the beach.

The sun had nearly set as they walked toward it, a slight breeze playing with Eliza's hair.

"All the time," he said. "But then I realize, I'm not someone else. This is what I've got to work with. And it might not be much, but maybe that's okay. Maybe I'm not supposed to solve world hunger or create a new invention that will change life as we know it. When I fix things, when I leave things better than when I arrived...I've made the world better for that person. And maybe that's enough. Maybe being a handyman is the way I'm meant to make the world a better place."

Eliza threw a glance his way. "That seems a little hypocritical."

"What do you mean?" He seemed genuinely confused.

"The other night, you said I shouldn't be happy with just going around town, doing odds and ends. You said I was letting fear hold me back—that I wasn't reaching my potential."

"Oh." And that was all Travis said, his brows scrunched up in concentration. "I guess I did say that, didn't I? And I shouldn't have. You're right."

Wow. A guy who could admit when he was wrong. That was something she didn't come across often. Maybe she'd been hanging out in the wrong places.

"So, which one is it? Should I feel disappointed because I'm not pushing myself toward my dreams, or should I be happy to help the town in the little ways I already am?"

Travis didn't say anything for a beat and ran his fingers through his hair before finally saying, "I don't know."

Great. So they were two people stuck in lives they hadn't meant to live, and not knowing if they should feel grateful or crappy about the way things had turned out. At least she had company.

They had reached the sand, and Eliza slipped her sandals off. The sand was cold against her toes, but she relished it. The chill woke her up and livened her senses. It had the same effect that running usually had for her, and she suddenly felt the need to take off and just go for it.

Travis was watching her, his lips twitching up at the corners. "You're bouncing like you're at the starting line, waiting for that gun to go off. I'll run with you, if you want company."

Eliza's gaze snapped toward him. No one had ever offered to run with her before. Usually they were trying to slow her down.

"I'm fast," she warned him.

He smiled. "I know. I'll try to keep up, but don't slow down for me."

Eliza returned his smile, her heart beating fast even though she hadn't started running yet. That was what Travis's smile did to her—that was what everything about him did to her.

And that made her nervous.

"You ready?" she asked, after setting her sandals down in the sand. She took her runner's stance, but Travis had already slipped off his shoes and taken off down the beach.

"Hey, no fair," she called after him, running to catch up.

"It is when I know you'll pass me no matter when I start," he called back, laughing. He was right, of course. Eliza easily caught up, but for once, she was okay with not passing him. She was okay with not winning, and not proving that she really was the fastest. And they ran, side by side, the wind nipping at their bare skin. They ran past the lifeguard station, past the locals who had decided to skip the town meeting in favor of the sunset stroll, and all the way to a giant rock at the opposite side of the beach.

The top of the rock had an overhang that tended to trap heat and make the air just that tiny bit warmer under it. It wasn't much, but it would be a good place to rest. Eliza didn't need it, but she could hear Travis's heavy breaths, and she wanted to give him a break without him having to ask for it.

"How you holding up?" she asked when they reached the overhang. She bent over and rested her hands on her knees, as if she were tired.

Travis couldn't answer as he tried to catch his breath and instead gave Eliza a weak thumbs up.

"Thank you," she said, plopping down in the cold sand. "For tonight. For the run. I needed this. And it was nice to not feel guilty about it."

"Who makes someone feel bad about going for a run?" he asked, his breaths still coming hard. He sat down in the sand next to her.

"People who tell me to slow down, that I'm already in good shape. That I don't need it. As if looking good is the sole reason that people exercise. Honestly, at this point, I run to keep sane."

"I get that. I play with wood as my outlet." He nodded toward the necklace Eliza wore. She hoped he mistook the pink in her cheeks as caused by exertion and not the attraction she felt toward him at that moment.

"You have a real talent," she said, fingering the necklace. "You could sell these, you know."

He lifted a shoulder and leaned back, propping himself up on his elbows. "Maybe. But then it wouldn't be for me anymore."

Eliza leaned back next to him, letting the sound of the waves wash over her. As much as this town drove her crazy, she couldn't imagine living anywhere else.

"Eliza?"

She glanced over and was startled to see the intensity behind Travis's eyes, even in the dark. "Yeah?"

"I really want to kiss you right now."

Eliza blinked. "Oh?"

"But I don't want this to be a rebound thing. I don't want to do it out of loneliness or frustration or confusion about what I'm doing with my life. Right now I want to kiss you because I like you. A lot."

That was...formal.

Even so, Eliza's stomach twisted and flipped in excitement. She had never had a man be this upfront before, and it was kind of refreshing being told where he stood in the relationship...or whatever this was.

But Travis wasn't finished yet.

He blew out a hard breath and sat up, pulling his knees into his chest, and looked out over the ocean. "I'm sorry, I don't mean to put pressure on you. That's not fair. It's just that...I don't want to wonder from day to day if you like me or if you hate me. Because, honestly, I'm never quite sure. Even after you kissed me the other night, I still didn't know. And if I kiss you tonight, if you kiss me back, I want it to mean the same thing."

Eliza sat up, watching him.

She knew that last statement was valid—but she also realized a startling truth. This guy, who had every woman in town chasing after him, was one of the most insecure men she'd ever met. He really didn't see how incredible he was. And how intimidating that could be for someone like Eliza. Travis had so many insecurities, it put Eliza's to shame.

"Travis," she said, placing a hand on his cheek and turning his gaze toward her. His eyes—they were troubled. Nervous. And then she realized she didn't know what to say. And as it turned out, she didn't need to.

Travis leaned in, catching her by surprise, and placed his lips gently on hers. His hand found its way to the back of her neck, and he shifted his weight so he could rest the other on her hip.

Eliza's breath caught in her chest. The guy had put an awful lot of meaning on this kiss and how she reacted to it. But in this moment, nothing mattered but his lips and his hands. So she pulled him in tighter, pressing herself against him. Their kiss deepened as their lips explored each other. She raked one hand through his short hair, and his breath hitched, making his kisses more frantic, like he couldn't get enough of her.

How long had it been since someone hadn't been able to get enough of her? Long enough that she pressed him down to the sand, and they stayed that way until long after she was freezing, but not caring. The only thing keeping her warm was him.

And she liked it that way.

## 19

Travis walked the boardwalk, whistling, his tool belt slung over one shoulder. He was like a walking advertisement for one of those medications where they always showed the happiest people on earth, right before disclosing that the medication could kill them.

Maybe what he had going with Eliza would be no different, but he didn't care. Because he was happy, and for once in his life, he wasn't afraid to admit it.

Spotting Adeline in her chocolate shop, he stepped in for a sample.

"One of these days you're going to buy something when you visit my store," she teased.

Travis smiled as she pulled out his usual chile chocolate truffle. Spicy and sweet with just the right balance. He paused, wondering if Eliza would like something from Adeline's shop. He knew Eliza tried to watch what she ate but also knew she liked to splurge on truffles now and again. "Actually, why don't we make that day today. I'll take a whole box."

Adeline's lips parted in surprise, and she laughed. "I should have spotted it the second you walked in here." She leaned back and called, "Honey, Travis finally succumbed. It took two weeks longer than you predicted, but the man has found someone."

Heat traveled up Travis's neck, and he spluttered, "A-a man can stock up on your world-famous truffles just because he likes them, can't he?"

Eli stuck his head around the corner. "Sure he can. Except, you never have. Until today, with you standing there grinning like a fool. So, who is she?"

Travis attempted a scowl at the actor, but he couldn't quite manage it. He could see why all the women, and men, gravitated toward Eli. Not only was he good-looking, he was a generally nice guy, and you couldn't help but like him.

"None of your business. So, if you don't mind?" He nodded toward the chile chocolates.

"Oh, hoh. None of my business, huh?" Adeline smirked as she grabbed a box of chocolates from the counter behind her. "We'll see about that."

Uh-oh. He'd challenged Adeline's small-town gossiping skills, and she had the look of someone who was bent on proving him wrong.

"Honey, do you mind ringing him up? I have a quick call I need to make."

Eli grinned and took her place behind the register. "Now you've done it. It took me a while after coming here too, but you learn quick when to hold your tongue."

"She's calling Jessie, isn't she?"

Elli nodded. "She's calling Jessie."

Travis tried paying and getting out of there before Adeline returned, but he wasn't quick enough.

"I don't believe it," Adeline said, her face practically glowing with excitement. "I mean, I knew it was weird that Jessie had bid on that date with you." She turned to her husband, who seemed just as eager for whatever gossip Adeline had as any of the women would be. Looked like Eli Hunt had gone full-time small town.

"Jessie bestowed her date on Eliza, who she wasn't sure would actually go. But then Eliza and Travis went out Saturday night. Jessie hadn't heard a thing since then, so she planted the seed for Travis to go to the town council meeting last night, where she knew Eliza would be. And from up front, Jessie saw them leave together. And they didn't come back. Nor was Eliza home when Jessie stopped by her house afterward to make sure she was okay. You know, with us not making quite as much money from the fundraiser as we had hoped for. Anyway, when I told her that Travis was in here whistling and buying chocolates, she almost lost her mind."

Adeline paused long enough to take a breath, then turned her attention to Travis. "Did I leave anything out?"

Travis's thoughts immediately went to him and Eliza kissing on the beach until their feet had gone numb, and then their run back to where they'd left their shoes. And then a little more kissing. Eventually he'd gotten Eliza back home. He could still feel her hands raking through his hair—her lips hungrily exploring his. And how he wanted to do it all over again, every day, forever.

"Um...no, I think you got it all."

Adeline gave a satisfied nod. "It's about time, for both of you."

Travis felt that was a bit unfair, considering he'd only been in town six weeks, but there was no use arguing with Adeline. She'd win.

So he told her thank you for the chocolates, and yes, he'd tell Eliza hello and congratulations. And no, they didn't have a wedding date.

Travis laughed as he left and made his way toward Eliza's house. On the way, he passed the florist shop and made another impromptu stop. Natalie, the owner, was standing behind the counter, working on an arrangement that was a mixture of daisies and roses. It didn't seem like the typical combination, but it worked well, the white contrasting with the red.

She brightened when the bell rang above the door and she saw it was him. Natalie was one of the few single women in town he wasn't terrified of, but his sights had settled elsewhere.

"Hi, Travis. Not used to seeing you in here unless there's a problem. Are you here as a handyman or as a customer?"

He returned her smile. "Customer. I'm looking for something special. Something that's romantic but not over the top, you know what I mean?"

She nodded, not showing the least bit of disappointment that he was buying flowers for another woman. Not that he would expect her to, but that just seemed to be the go-to reaction for most of the women in town. "I think I have just what you're looking for. And it's on the house. Really, I can't thank you enough for fixing that leaky pipe in my apartment last week."

"You don't need to do that. I can pay for the flowers. But you know those pipes are a ticking time bomb. They're fine for now, but they won't last forever. You need to get them replaced before they burst and do some real damage."

Natalie reached into a display fridge behind her. "I appreciate the warning, and I will get to it, I promise. It's just a busy time of year, you know? You'd be surprised at how many of these tourists get themselves into the doghouse on vacation and need a quick trip to the florist. It's astounding, is what it is."

When she turned back to him, she held a vase.

"I'm going to tell you what each of these are so that you'll sound super thoughtful when you give them to her, okay?"

He nodded in agreement, because other than the roses, he didn't have the slightest clue what he'd be giving Eliza. All he knew was that it was perfect.

"Peach-colored roses surrounded by white lilies and mini

peach-colored carnations. Don't worry about the greenery that accents them. She won't ask." Natalie smiled and handed the vase over. "And I was serious about them being on the house. You and Eliza deserve the best."

So, she already knew. Word traveled fast. All it had taken was a two-block walk from Adeline's chocolate shop. He'd need to warn Eliza.

"Thank you," he said, while placing a twenty on the counter. "And I was serious about paying for them."

Natalie laughed but took the money. She had shown typical Starlight Ridge hospitality, and he had shown it right back. Looked like he was learning to play the game after all.

By the time Travis reached Eliza's house, he was nervous that he'd gone over the top. Was he doing too much too fast, acting like the committed boyfriend, when they hadn't actually placed a title on their relationship? And really, chocolates and flowers? A bit cliché much?

Too late now, the damage had been done. Even if he chose not to give Eliza the gifts, she'd know that he'd bought them for her. He'd actually be surprised if she didn't already know.

He knocked.

No noise from inside.

Travis tried the doorbell.

Same result.

Eliza was constantly being sent all over town for odd jobs, so she could be anywhere, and he didn't really want to leave the gifts on her doorstep.

"You looking for Eliza?"

Travis turned to find Erwin standing on the sidewalk, holding a leash, a beautiful dog pulling against the resistance, trying to get him moving.

No use pretending he wasn't there for Eliza. "Yeah. Do you know where she is?"

"Lifeguard station. Just passed her as we walked the beach."

Travis nodded his thanks and walked back the way he'd come, grateful he was heading in a different direction than the older man. Not that there was anything wrong with Erwin. It was just that he was as bad as Jessie when it came to probing questions that Travis would rather not answer.

"So, you and Eliza, huh?" Erwin asked anyway.

"Just a friendly visit."

Travis kept walking.

"That's not what your chocolate and flowers are saying. It's not what Adeline's saying either, according to Jessie."

"Time will tell, Erwin," Travis called over his shoulder. He didn't slow down.

By the time he'd reached the beach, beads of sweat had formed on his brow. He chalked it up to the warm day, but he'd also noticed his muscles had lost some definition. Life as a handyman was taking its toll, and he'd have to do better if he wanted to keep up with Eliza.

With his arms full, Travis couldn't slip off his shoes, so he dealt with the warm sand spilling inside, making its way into his socks and rubbing against his bare skin. But he made it to the lifeguard station, and to Eliza sitting there above him, keeping an eagle eye out for any tourists who made the mistake of swimming too far or entering the ocean in the wrong spot.

"You look good up there."

Eliza jumped, startled, and then laughed. "Thank you. It's a hard job, but someone has to do it."

He smiled and held out the flowers and chocolates toward her. "These are for you, something to help the time go by a little faster."

Pink crept into her cheeks as she took the gifts and then glanced around, as if to check if anyone was watching.

"Oh, you're okay with liking me in the dark, but not so much out here, huh?" he teased, but even he could admit he felt awkward. He'd meant to give them to her at home, away from prying eyes. "I stopped by your house, and you weren't there. Sorry."

Eliza's attention returned to him, and she quickly said, "Oh no, that's not it at all. Thank you. I've just never had anyone surprise me with flowers. And in public. But it's definitely not a bad thing." She flashed a smile, and then her gaze dropped, like she was embarrassed and didn't know how to continue.

"If it helps you feel any better, the entire town knows that something is happening here, and they made sure I knew it everywhere I went for the past hour." He paused. That sounded presumptuous, didn't it. "I mean, *if* there's something going on. They suspect. I know we haven't said exactly what's happening, but Adeline told Jessie I was buying chocolates, and then Jessie confirmed that we went out, and then Natalie said she heard from Jessie, and somehow Erwin found out, so I figured I should probably warn you and...yeah. I'm going to stop there."

Eliza swept her gaze over the ocean as if making sure that everyone was exactly where they should be, and then she jumped from the lifeguard station and gave him a quick kiss. "They can talk all they want, but just to make sure we're on the same page, something is definitely going on here. And I love the chocolate and flowers. Thank you." One more kiss and a mischievous smile later, she climbed back onto her seat, her gaze returning to the ocean.

"Will you do me a favor?" she asked, glancing down. "Would you mind asking Natalie to save these in her fridge for me until I get home?" She nodded toward the flowers. "I still have another couple of hours, and those things will never survive out here in the heat."

Travis smiled. "Sure. And the chocolates?"

"Oh, I'm keeping those. I'll need them to survive those two hours."

Travis turned to leave with the flowers, but as he did, Eliza said, "Travis?"

He glanced back.

"Can I cook you dinner tonight? I have no idea what's in the fridge, but I always come up with something." She seemed eager to spend more time with him, and even the prospect made his breaths quicken. But he didn't want that to become the relationship—they both work hard all day and then she comes home and feels like she has to cook.

"I'll tell you what, I have a few jobs to do, but when I'm done, how about I cook for you instead? Sitting out here in the sun, saving lives, is going to leave you far more exhausted than me replacing a few hinges."

Eliza seemed surprised but then nodded, her face nearly splitting from the smile that had exploded across her face.

A smile that he'd been able to put there.

He hoped he could continue to surprise her—to be able to make her smile.

Travis couldn't imagine anything better.

## 20

Eliza didn't know what she'd done to deserve someone like Travis, but the universe had smiled down on her. After all these years, she had found someone who hadn't tried to change her. Someone who didn't want anything from her. Someone who just...let her be.

She watched as Travis bustled around the kitchen, throwing what seemed to be random ingredients into a pan.

"Need any help over there?" she asked from where she sat at a small folding table that had been pushed against the opposite wall. The dining room/living room was small, and it was fine for a single person, or even a couple. Eliza didn't know how Bree and Caleb did it in a similarly sized apartment with a new baby, though.

"No, I'm fine. Just figuring things out. I had plans to make something Thai, but Mueller Market is a bit lacking when it comes to international foods."

That was an understatement.

"Yeah. If I had known, I could have warned you."

Travis pulled a bottle from the fridge and threw in a dash of a dark liquid. "They did have fish sauce, though, and I figured out some substitutions. Hopefully it will still be good."

She leaned against the wall and watched as he worked. "You sure I can't help?"

He shot her a smile. "Wouldn't be enough room in here for the two of us, even if I said yes."

Another true statement. But Eliza wouldn't mind the close proximity.

"Where'd you learn how to cook?" she asked.

"Mostly Thailand, but I did some traveling before that. Although, I have to say, compared to what I'm doing right now, cooking in Thailand is way easier."

"Why's that?"

Travis glanced over. "Because people there don't expect you to follow a recipe." And then he released a cannon-like laugh, and Eliza couldn't help but laugh with him. "You have your meats and your vegetables and sauces. And sure, each dish has certain things that go in it, but I never once saw a measuring cup or spoons."

"Sounds like my kind of place. I'd love to go there someday."

Travis paused for a beat, then kept moving. "It's beautiful."

"Do you think you'll ever go back?"

He raised a shoulder. "Maybe. If I had a reason to." And then he shot another glance her way.

Meaning Travis could return with Eliza. Or was she over-thinking this?

Was she ready for that type of commitment?

It wasn't like they were getting married, she had to remind herself. Nothing was tying her down. She was just having fun. Enjoying herself, for the first time ever.

Eliza looked out the window at all the tourists moving around down there, as if they didn't have a care in the world.

Starlight Ridge was their happy place—the place they visited so they could pretend.

Why couldn't it be that for Eliza too?

"The volleyball competition starts this weekend," she said, returning her attention to Travis. "If we do well, I'll be gone most weekends. Except for when we host in two weeks. Then the craziness you see now will triple."

"That's great." Travis cut up a bell pepper and threw it into the sizzling pan. "Are you excited?"

"I should be. I was."

He took the pan off the stove and let it continue to cook while he pulled out two plates. "What changed?"

Eliza hesitated. "I told you before that I'm not passionate about sports. The truth is, I don't even like them. At all. Especially team sports. And beach volleyball is my least favorite yet."

Travis's gaze snapped to hers, and he held it, disbelief etched in his features. "Are you serious?"

She gave a small nod, heat traveling up her neck and into her cheeks. Eliza knew it was ridiculous. But not liking volleyball had never bothered her before. It had just been another way to focus her energy.

"I don't like the way the sand gets into every crevice," she said with an embarrassed smile. "And it's not like the women on my team care if we win or lose. They're just trying to have some fun and get a break from their families. At least when it's competition season, it's like a girls' trip every weekend."

Travis looked away and busied himself dishing the food out onto the plates. "If you don't like it, why do it? There has to be something else you can do—something you actually enjoy."

Yes, that would be the reasonable course of action, wouldn't it? "I'm more of a racquetball or tennis type of woman. I could also definitely see myself running marathons. But I do what's available, you know. I try to change it up every so often, and until recently, I've been fine with that."

Travis didn't respond to that, the plates of food having completely absorbed his attention, not even a glance her way. He had to know that he had turned her world upside down. That she didn't understand anything anymore. That the things that used to hold her together were no longer sufficient.

All because of him.

And that realization scared her. Because there was no guarantee that Travis would always be there. No guarantee that she would either.

She couldn't let a guy who happened to cook and liked to surprise her with handmade wooden necklaces and flowers and chocolate truffles throw her for a loop. Because she knew what she had to do—and why she had to do it.

Eliza had never expected it to be easy.

"I don't know," she finally said. "I'm still figuring things out. What I do know is that I would much rather be spending my weekends with you than traveling all over the state with women who talk about parenting tips the entire time."

Travis brought over two steaming plates of what look like beef and vegetables in a dark sauce with rice to the side. It smelled spicy and amazing.

"This is my type of meal," she said, tossing him a smile.

He returned the smile and sat down. "Healthy yet satisfying." He blew on a spoonful of food that looked way too hot for immediate consumption. "I bet you still have fun on your weekends, though, right? Even if you aren't living the same life as the other women."

Eliza blew on her own spoonful of food. "Yeah, I do. I'm sorry, I don't mean to complain. I'm very grateful for my team and the opportunities I've had." A brief pause. "Do you want to come with me? To the competition this weekend, I mean."

Eliza hadn't planned on inviting Travis, it had just kind of burst out.

His head tilted to the side, and he studied her, his smile morphing into questioning amusement. "You really want me there?"

Eliza paused and really thought about it for the first time. "Yes, but at the same time, you'd be the only man there with a bunch of women. That probably wouldn't be much fun for you, would it?"

"I was thinking it would be more awkward for them," he said with a laugh. "Not that I don't appreciate the invite. How about if I wait until you are competing here in Starlight Ridge? I'd love to see you play."

"You got a taste of it your first day in town. Remember that?"

Travis leaned back in his chair as he chewed, and rested his hands on his stomach. "That I do."

As they ate and chatted, Eliza couldn't imagine being there with anyone else. Travis made her laugh until she cried, and then she actually cried because the food was so spicy, she had tears rolling down her cheeks and her nose was running. But she kept eating because it was so delicious, in spite of Travis handing her a tissue and telling her she could stop anytime and he wouldn't judge.

That was before he snapped a picture with his phone and told her that she was at her most beautiful right then, which Eliza was tempted to be offended by. The crying, snotty, red-faced Eliza that he'd captured was not the one she wanted to be remembered as.

All the same, it made her heart beat faster and her head feel woozy. This was a man who saw good in her, at every moment. And was completely genuine about it.

It was after dinner, the dishes done, when they were cuddled on the couch, that they made their boldest decision yet.

They were going to go down to the sunset stroll together. In public. Where everyone could see, and rumors could fly.

Even though Travis and Eliza could see the sunset from the hardware store window, it wasn't the same as being out on the beach with the rest of the town. Besides, with so many tourists out and about, Travis and Eliza would easily blend in. Go unnoticed. They'd be able to enjoy the evening, gossip-free.

Wishful thinking, Eliza knew. But hey, it could happen.

It didn't happen.

The moment they stepped out on the beach, Patty spotted them and made a beeline toward where they were slipping off their shoes. She started by commenting on how lovely it was to see the two of them there together. Harmless enough stuff. But then Patty stopped mid-sentence, looked them up and down, placed her hands on her hips, and turned a fierce gaze on Travis.

"Boy, you better take that woman's hand in yours right now. Inviting Eliza here and then keeping three feet between you is no way to help her feel loved."

Travis's mouth opened and closed, like he really didn't know what to say to that. He looked to Eliza for help, but she had none to give and merely smiled and shrugged like, *What am I going to do about it?*

So he turned back to Patty and said, "Yes, ma'am." And he took Eliza's hand, interlacing his fingers with hers. He held their hands up and asked, "Better?"

Patty nodded in satisfaction. "Better." And then, as if her work was done, she wandered off, no doubt to tell everyone that she'd caught Travis and Eliza there, holding hands.

Sometimes the gossip in Starlight Ridge was less gossip and more self-fulfilling prophecy.

But Travis didn't let go of Eliza's hand when Patty was out of sight. Instead, his thumb caressed the side of her hand, sending chills. Eliza knew they'd kissed before—more than once. And it had been amazing. But it had been different than this. Kissing... making out...it was an act of attraction, to be sure, but also passion.

This was the first time they'd ever touched each other in public. And hand-holding, it was more familiar...more intimate, somehow.

It meant something.

"I'm sorry it took Patty to get me to hold your hand," he whispered as they pushed through the crowd to an area that was less populated. "I would have gotten around to it tonight, promise."

Eliza felt her attraction to this man growing every day, and that passion that came with kissing? It was eating her up right now, begging her to take him down to the sand. But because this was neither the time nor the place, and there were children around, she fought the smile that begged to take over her entire face and said, "I believe you."

Travis pulled her by the hand so they were close enough to the ocean that the waves threatened to lap onto their feet, but then would roll back out just in time. He turned to face Eliza, taking both of her hands in his.

"You know that feeling when you're a teenager, and you're at the movie theater, and you place your hand on the edge of your seat, hoping that your date will get the hint and place theirs similarly? And it takes the first half of the movie for your hands to slowly inch towards each other, one thumb eventually brushing up against the other, and you finally take courage to place your hand on theirs? But the movie is basically over by that point?"

Eliza nodded, knowing that feeling very well. The excitement of the moment, however brief.

Travis sucked in a quick breath, like he was nervous. "That's how I feel around you—like I'm a teenager, not knowing how to act. Hoping you like me as much as I like you. Still unsure if it's okay that I hold your hand or bring you flowers. I get butterflies in my stomach when you walk into a room, and I wonder if you'll sit in the seat that I left open for you."

"The seat at the town meeting. It was for me." Eliza felt dumb for not realizing it sooner. Even after she'd been angry with him and wouldn't talk to him...he'd still saved a seat for her.

Travis gave her an embarrassed smile. "Yeah, it was." That had been the first night they'd kissed. She didn't count their date night. The night of the town meeting—that had been a good night.

Eliza squeezed both of his hands and stepped closer. "Thank you. For giving me a chance."

"Always."

And then they kissed. Which would have been totally romantic, if not for a little boy yelling, "Ew, they're kissing."

Laughter.

Eliza pulled away, her cheeks burning up.

It wouldn't have mattered if it had just been the nearby tourists who had overheard. But then Eliza heard, "Erwin, did you see that. They're finally together." That was Jessie. "You owe me fifty bucks."

"I said they'd be together by the end of the week," he protested.

"That was last week."

"I didn't specify the end of *which* week."

Eliza groaned and buried her face in Travis's chest, and he wrapped his arms around her, laughing.

"Guess we're officially dating," he said. "Exactly how a couple of awkward teenagers would have done it. They wouldn't have a 'define the relationship' conversation. Their friends would do it for them, and that would be that."

Eliza leaned back and kissed him once quickly on the chin, because that was as high as she could reach. "So, just to be clear —and yes, I still insist on having a define-the-relationship conversation—can I call you my boyfriend?"

She threw him a grin to show that she was teasing him.

Travis matched her grin and brought her in for another kiss. "Yes, you can call me your boyfriend."

"Good."

And then they heard Erwin say, "It's official, he's her boyfriend. Job well done, folks. Job well done."

And then Jessie. "What? I can't hear you over all these people."

So Erwin yelled it this time. "He's her boyfriend!"

## 21

Travis had never felt lighter than these past couple of weeks. Of course, he missed Eliza like crazy when she was away for her volleyball competition that first weekend, but then she was back, and he took every chance he could to see her.

Rather than Eliza running alone in the mornings, he ran with her. She could certainly have gone faster and further if she'd been alone, but she didn't seem to mind. Half the time they ended up walking for long sections, talking, holding hands. Laughing. Lots of laughing.

The things couples did. The things he'd missed out on for so long.

And he couldn't imagine doing it with anyone but Eliza.

Which was amazing, because he'd thought she was exactly the type of woman he didn't need in his life.

And that no one could have compared to Chloe.

He no longer thought of his unrequited love. Chloe could have Davis. Because Travis had found something better.

Someone he didn't have to beg to return his feelings. Someone who enjoyed his company, whether they were talking, or running, or reading side by side, or kissing. It didn't matter.

The town gossip had settled down and they had become old news, which was fine by him. That left more chances for them to steal away, be normal.

Travis had always thought that once he was in a serious relationship, it would quickly spiral into monotony—doing the same thing day in and day out. No more surprises.

But with Eliza, it was one surprise after another. Which was why he *wasn't* surprised to wake up to a text from Eliza one morning telling him that she had taken off work, had made sure everyone knew that Travis wouldn't be available, and was stealing him away for the day. It was followed by an emoji blowing kisses.

He grinned and jumped out of bed, ready to jog over to Eliza's house. But he then realized he had no idea if he should eat breakfast, how long they'd be gone, or what type of clothes he should wear.

And when he called to find out, all he was told was that, yes, he should eat breakfast, Eliza didn't know how long they'd be gone, and he could wear anything he liked as long as it wasn't a tux.

Eliza picked him up at the hardware store forty-five minutes later...in a car, of all things. Travis didn't remember the last time he'd actually driven somewhere.

This must be a special day.

"I don't get any hints?" he asked Eliza after giving her a quick kiss and sliding into the car.

She smiled as he buckled his seatbelt. "You keep up with the kisses, and I suppose I could arrange some hints along the way."

"I feel like that's bribery."

Eliza laughed and said, "Uh-huh." She lowered her window, and a warm breeze flowed through the car as she pulled out and wound her way out of Starlight Ridge. Eliza had always been beautiful, but right now, she was gorgeous—happy. Like a weight had lifted and she was free.

Travis took her right hand and kissed it. "I'm ready for my first hint."

"I brought food."

Okay, not what he had been expecting. But food was always good.

He tapped his chin as if pondering what that could mean. "You brought your own food, which means we will be somewhere that doesn't have a restaurant nearby. So...some kind of nature thing?"

Eliza threw a grin his way. "You're good. Too good. No more hints for you."

"Aw, come on. Please?" He turned her hand over and kissed the palm this time. Travis knew that she liked that especially, and her resolve seemed to weaken. But then she steeled up.

"Nope. Sorry."

He smiled and gently kissed her wrist. "Are you sure?" He then kissed just above her wrist, and then further up her arm, and then a little further, until Eliza squealed and stole her arm back.

"If you keep this up, you are going to make us get into an accident." She was grinning, though, so not mad.

"Why, because I'm so irresistible?" Travis batted his eyes.

"Yes. That's exactly why."

Travis released a dramatic sigh and leaned back in his seat. "Fine. No more kisses. I get it. From now on, this right here," he used his hand to draw an imaginary circle around his face, "is a kiss-free zone."

Eliza's jaw dropped in mock horror. "Now, hold on a minute. I think you misunderstood."

"Oh, no, I understand perfectly. And don't worry. It's fine. I get it."

The thing with Eliza was that Travis had learned to expect the unexpected from her. But what he hadn't expected was for her to abruptly pull over to the side of the road, put the car in park, squeeze out from under the steering wheel, and jump onto his lap—which was a feat in her tiny car.

Travis did everything he could to keep a straight face. "I'm sorry, I'm only following orders."

Eliza scrunched up her nose. "I rescind your orders and give you new ones. Kiss me."

"Nope."

"Fine. You don't have to do a thing." And then Eliza wrapped her arms around him and placed her lips on his, her fingers playing with his hair. Travis held out as long as he could, but what felt like an eternity turned out to only be about ten seconds or so.

Eliza was right to say she had no idea when they'd be returning to Starlight Ridge. As she slid her hand along Travis's chest and his breath hitched, he decided he'd be okay if they never returned.

They had food, apparently. And each other. What else did they need?

"I WAS HAVING doubts you even had a destination in mind," Travis teased as he stepped out of the car and stretched his legs.

Eliza laughed. "What, you thought the plan was to drive to the middle of nowhere so we could make out, when we could have done the same thing at home?"

He lifted a shoulder. "I'm just saying, I would be okay with that plan."

She leaned over the hood of the car, pulled him in by his

shirt, and planted a long kiss on him. "I'm saving up for the ride home."

Oh, yeah. They were definitely not going to make it home any time soon.

Eliza laughed again and shook her head. "I can see what you're thinking, you know."

He really needed to work on that transparency thing.

Travis leaned against the car, tilting his face to the sun, as Eliza opened the trunk and pulled out a basket.

"You up for a seaside picnic?" she asked, holding the basket up for him to see.

"Sure, sounds great." What Travis didn't say was that, yet again, this was something they could have done at home, as opposed to driving an hour and a half up the coast. Not that he was complaining.

"I know, I know, we've had plenty of seaside picnics back home," Eliza said, once again reading him like an open book. "But this place is something special."

At this point, Travis wouldn't have cared even if it wasn't. Just getting away for the day and spending it with Eliza was enough. But he gave her a lopsided grin and said, "Show me what you got."

They were parked in a small lot off the coastal road, but when Travis looked toward the ocean, rather than seeing waves crashing against the shore, there was a large inlet. Nestled inside the inlet's rocky shore, the water was calm and had a bluish-green tint to it. It was breathtaking.

Eliza was right—this was worth the drive.

Travis held out a hand to take the basket from Eliza as they made their way toward a rocky path that led toward the water, but she gave him a look that said, *Really?* and lifted the basket above her head a few times like a barbell to show that she could handle carrying their food a few yards.

He laughed and gave a shrug that said, *It was worth a try.*

"It's beautiful," he said, pausing to take in the scenery before him. That was when he noticed a green head break the water's surface, then disappear again. His gaze snapped to Eliza. "Was that—"

She grinned. "A Pacific green turtle. Yes, they are why we're here."

Travis walked slowly now, making his way down the path and toward the water's edge. Another head broke the surface, then disappeared. His gaze scanned the rocky shore, and for the first time, he noticed turtles sunbathing on rocks on the oppo site side.

"Are they here year-round?" he asked, turning to Eliza.

She set the picnic basket down on a large rock and began pulling items from it. "They nest in Mexico, but when they aren't there, yes, they migrate up the California coast." She unfolded a small blanket that she laid over the rock, then set out plates and sandwiches. "I went classic with ham and cheese."

"Sounds great. You shouldn't mess with the classics."

Eliza gave a serious nod. "My thoughts exactly. We also have pickles, carrots, grape tomatoes, chips, cookies, tarts...and there's probably something else in here. I don't know, Jessie helped me pack."

Oh, that was interesting. Jessie had helped Eliza pack for their date. Travis was unsure what to make of that.

Once again, his transparency gave him away.

Eliza handed a plate to Travis and smiled. "She didn't see me on my daily run this morning and stopped by to make sure everything was okay. When I told her what I was up to, she immediately went home and returned with all sorts of things to send along. She also wanted me to tell you hi and to not worry about your store, she'll keep an eye on everything."

Yes, that sounded like Jessie.

"Thank you," he said, playing with the edge of his sandwich but not yet eating. "Seriously. For all of this. For...you." He blew out a breath and ran a hand through his hair. Travis didn't know how to put into words what Eliza had come to mean to him. He'd come a long way since that first day when her volleyball had nailed him in the head.

"I could say the same thing to you," she said, her voice quiet. "I don't know if I've ever laughed as much as I have since meeting you. I had nearly forgotten what that was like."

His lips quirked up at the corners. He knew the feeling. "I know I haven't been in Starlight Ridge for long—only a couple of months. But—"

Eliza laid her plate on the rock next to her and scooted in closer, her gaze expectant.

Travis hesitated, but this was the only way to convey to Eliza how deep his feelings ran. "I love you, Eliza. I thought I knew love before, but it didn't come close to what I feel for you. You motivate me to be better...stronger. Kinder. Every day, my goal is to be the man that you deserve."

A wave of insecurity suddenly crashed over Travis. He shouldn't have just laid it all out like that. He was going to scare her off.

And then Eliza's eyes filled with moisture.

Oh, crap. He'd made her cry. That was so much worse.

But then she said, her voice thick with emotion, "I love you too. So, so much. I wasn't living life before you came along— merely surviving. Do you know how long it's been since I've been to this bay? Years. I don't even know an exact number— that's how long it's been. I never allowed myself to slow down enough to live in the moment. You've given me that, and so much more."

She loved him.

Eliza Meyer was in love with Travis.

Armed with this new knowledge, Travis spent the next two hours cuddled up on that rock with Eliza, watching the turtles, and eating ham and cheese sandwiches.

And knowing that life didn't get much better than this.

## 22

It had been one week since Eliza had whisked Travis off to Turtle Bay. One week since she'd told him she loved him. One week since life had seemed more perfect than she'd ever imagined it could be.

She should have known it was too good to be true.

Because, one week later, Eliza now stared at the piece of paper in front of her—the results from her latest blood test. For the past decade, every three months, Eliza had come into Patty's office and had her blood tested. It was routine by now, and she never missed. Had to stay on top of things.

These results...they weren't horrible. But they weren't good either.

"I don't understand," she said, her gaze snapping up to Patty's. "My results have been the same for three years. I got them down to a good level, and they've been steady. Always the same. I tweak a little as necessary, but it's the healthiest my heart has ever been. How could the numbers rise like this, after so long?"

Patty held out her hands, as if to say *Don't shoot the messenger.* "Have your habits changed? What is your diet like?"

She shook her head. "It's the same as it's always been. I eat healthy, maybe a few truffles now and again. I couldn't exercise for a few days when I had the flu, but I wasn't really eating either."

Her thoughts flew to the frozen waffles she'd scarfed down, but they weren't super high in saturated fats. They were the expensive kind that were high protein, whole wheat. The syrup was one hundred percent natural, so even though not necessarily healthy, not as bad as it could have been.

Then there were the few seaside picnics she'd had with Travis, but a ham sandwich once in a while shouldn't have caused this drastic a change.

"So...*nothing* has changed?" Patty was looking at Eliza like she was getting at something but wanted Eliza to figure it out for herself.

Eliza lifted both shoulders and held out her hands. "What?" She wasn't in the mood for guessing games.

"A new relationship?"

"Oh, well, that doesn't have anything to do with anything," she said with a small laugh, and waved a hand through the air. "Travis cooks healthy dinners for me. He goes running with me. If anything, Travis is helping me stick to my goals. I enjoy going out and exercising now. My stress has reduced. He's been good for me."

Patty smiled. "I agree. You've found balance in your life that wasn't there before. He's very good for you. But you have to understand that with balance, other things have to give."

Eliza didn't understand what Patty was getting at. "Meaning?"

"Meaning that when you run with Travis is the mornings, are you pushing yourself as hard as you used to? When you practice with your volleyball team, are you as intense as you were? With your diet, are you making more exceptions than you used to?"

Eliza hadn't thought of it like that. She was still going out and doing all the activities, but she'd actually slowed down and started enjoying them.

But that was the whole point, wasn't it? She had slowed down.

Yes, Eliza was still in amazing shape and could outrun everyone else in town. Yes, she was still the strongest. Yes, she still ate the healthiest. But she wasn't as strong. She wasn't as healthy. Not like she had been before Travis had come into her life.

Before he'd helped her find her happy place.

"Are you saying I need to choose between my literal heart and the figurative one I've given to Travis?" Eliza asked, her voice breaking. That wasn't a choice she could make.

"Not at all." Patty sat in a chair next to Eliza and took her hand. "What I'm saying is that you deserve the happiness that Travis has brought into your life. You deserve to be with someone good and kind. And it's okay if you slow down to enjoy the journey with him. You *should* slow down."

"But it will affect my numbers."

Patty raised a shoulder in concession. "Yes, but these aren't horrible numbers. And isn't sacrificing in this area worth what you'll gain in every other area?"

Eliza's thoughts immediately flew to her mom. Her mother had given everything for their family. She had given love and joy...and her health. In the end, even though her mom had thought she was doing everything right, it hadn't been enough.

Her mom had had happiness, yes. And she'd thought it was worth it for what their family had. But then her mom's departure had created a hole in their family—a crater that Eliza's dad had never been able to crawl out of.

It had torn their family to shreds, and they'd never recovered.

And Eliza had stupidly thought she could have it all. How could she have been so naive?

"Thank you," she said, tears blinding her as she grabbed her purse. "I'll see you again in three months."

And then she hurried from the doctor's office.

Eliza didn't know how she was going to tell Travis it was over, but the longer she waited, the harder it would be. Maybe even impossible. And she couldn't do that to him.

FOUR DAYS until the volleyball game that would take place in Starlight Ridge. Four days to work their hardest and do their hometown proud.

Eliza showed up thirty minutes early to get in a quick run and stretch. The rest of the women showed up five minutes late, laughing and teasing each other. In the past few weeks, Eliza had loosened up, not been as strict. Had even joined in on the fun, turning their practices more into a social function.

Not anymore. They had barely won the previous weekend, and it had been so close that Eliza wasn't even sure they had been better than the other team. Just luckier. They had work to do.

"Gather up, ladies," she called. "We did well last weekend, but we can do better. We *need* to do better. That trophy has been just out of reach, but we're going to go all the way this year."

Bree and the others exchanged confused glances, like they didn't recognize her—didn't understand the words coming out of her mouth.

"Everything okay, Eliza?" Bree asked.

Eliza set her hands on her hips, the volleyball resting under one arm. "Of course. But considering that we're in the middle of a coast-wide competition, we kind of need to step it up a notch, don't you think?"

Bree hesitated. "Well, yes. But last week, you said we'd play better if we were having fun while doing it."

Oh, yeah. She had said that. One of those dumb things that people say when they are in love. When they think life is perfect and nothing could ever go wrong.

Eliza loved Travis more than she'd loved anyone since her mother. And that was why that evening, she was going to go to Travis's apartment to break his heart.

It was going to be broken eventually, so she might as well do it now when it would do less damage. Not after ten years of marriage and a child.

"I changed my mind."

Bree's expression was uneasy, but she gave a slow nod and said to the rest of the women, "All right. You heard her, bring it in." As if she were in charge.

Eliza set them straight that day, pushing them harder than she ever had. By the end of that hour, everyone was breathing hard, their faces red from exertion. And they were giving her a look of pure resentment. Like they would rather die than ever come to another volleyball practice.

"You did well today," she told them. "Play like that on Saturday, and the whole town will be carrying you on their shoulders."

But no one responded or would even look at her. Just trudged toward home so they could shower before the real work for the day began.

Everyone except Bree.

"That was intense, even for you," she said, hanging back. "Everything okay with Travis?"

Eliza forced her emotions down—wouldn't let them bubble up. Because if they did, they'd boil over. And she couldn't have that right now. This wasn't about emotions. It was about survival.

"Yeah, sure. Everything's fine. Just working some things out."

Bree nodded slowly and turned to go. "Mind working them out before practice tomorrow morning?" she said over her shoulder. "Because one more day like today, and I don't know if anyone is going to continue showing up to practices, let alone the game on Saturday."

And then she worked her way back to the scuba shop to help Caleb get ready for the day.

How did Bree get so lucky? She had a husband and a kid and her own photography business that she ran out of the scuba shop. And she didn't have to worry about tradeoffs. It was okay for her to just have fun playing volleyball, not worrying about whether she was the best at it. She didn't have to worry about if she was allowed to both be happy and live a long life.

Eliza trudged over to the lifeguard station, ready to take over for Isaac.

She wished the day was already over, and simultaneously that the evening would never come.

Because she did not want to do what had to be done.

## 23

Travis glanced at his phone as he tossed grilled chicken onto a bed of greens. A new text from Eliza. He loved getting the random text throughout the day, the ones that said *Thinking of you* or just had the little yellow emoji that was blowing kisses. They made the day go by faster until he could see her again.

But this one was different. There were no emojis. Just a quick message that said, *Can't make it for dinner. Go for a run with me later?*

She must have been called for a last-minute job in town. He looked at all the food he'd already been preparing. Maybe she'd be hungry after the run. At the very least, he'd have leftovers for a few days.

An hour later Travis walked down to the beach where Eliza was already stretching. He smiled at how serious she looked— like she was ready to take on the world.

"If you need a serious dose of protein after this, I have plenty of food back home," he said, coming up behind her and giving her a quick kiss on the neck.

Eliza stiffened.

That was not her usual reaction to his kisses.

"Thanks, but I think I'm good," she said, not turning around. "Ready to run?"

Okay, looked like it would be all business tonight.

"Yeah, sure." He slipped off his shoes, as usual, and took off running down the beach. That was when Eliza usually called him a cheater for getting a head start and she'd catch up, playfully pushing him into the water.

It never happened.

Instead, Eliza ran so hard and so fast, she was already halfway down the beach before Travis realized what was happening.

"Hey, wait up, Turbo," he called after her, but he doubted she'd heard.

Something was off tonight—something he hadn't yet encountered with Eliza. Maybe she'd had a bad day and needed to blow off some steam. Travis doubted he'd done anything wrong—he hadn't had the chance to.

Travis didn't manage to catch up with Eliza until he got to the rock outcropping at the other side of the beach. Oh, so that was why she had been in such a hurry. He smiled, thinking of the night of the auction when they'd made out in this same location, under the stars. That had been the night when he'd experienced something that had long alluded him—hope.

"Hey, next time you're in a hurry to kiss me on the beach, let me know first. I would have run faster," he said, teasing.

But Eliza didn't return his smile. Instead, his words caused the opposite reaction. Moisture pooled in her eyes, and she wiped it away, her lips forming a tight line, as if sheer willpower would dry her tears.

"What's wrong?" he asked, taking a step toward her. She mirrored him with a step back.

Okay, maybe he *had* done something.

"I'm not going to apologize until I know what I did."

Eliza's fists clenched. "Please don't make this harder than it already is."

Oh. So that was what this was. A breakup.

And suddenly Travis's world felt like it was crashing down around him. For the first time in a very long time, he'd been happy. He'd given his heart to someone—he'd never thought he'd be able to do that again.

But once again, for no apparent reason, he wasn't good enough.

He'd never known what the missing element had been with Chloe, just that there had been one. And once again, he found himself in the dark.

Travis sat on the sand and turned toward the ocean, pulling his knees to his chest. The sun was nearly gone, the moon taking its place, its image reflected on the water. So beautiful. And yet so sad. "Please don't tell me that it's you, not me," he said, his voice soft. "Because that's never true."

"In this case, it is." Her voice choked up. "I had my regular bloodwork done and got the results yesterday. It's not good."

His gaze whipped to Eliza. She leaned against the rock, her arms folded across her chest. Like that rock was the only thing holding her up.

Travis jumped to his feet and hurried to her side. "What can I do? Do you need to rest? What do you mean by 'not good?' You can get a second opinion, right?"

Eliza shook her head. "Rest is the last thing I need. In fact, the last few weeks, I've been doing too much of that."

The last few weeks. "You mean since we started seeing each other. You're saying that this is my fault."

Travis took a step back.

"It's not your fault," she insisted, but didn't try to close the gap between them. "I just don't push myself like I did... I allowed emotions to get in the way."

He gave her a sad smile. "You say that like it's a bad thing."

Eliza didn't respond for a minute, but then straightened, like she'd made up her mind about something. "My father knew about the heart problems that were on my mom's side of the family. So many of my relatives have died young from it, but he loved my mother and didn't care. And she him." Her lips twitched up into a smile. "He was the sheriff here, and he arrested my mom when she showed up on the beach with prescription medication that wasn't hers. She'd run away from home and taken her dad's medicine, knowing he could get more. My mom had the same prescription and wanted to make sure she had enough to get by until she figured things out."

That seemed like an odd story to tell at a time like this, but Travis was curious where she was going with it.

She glanced up. "My mom did everything right, did everything the doctor told her to, but she still left behind a grieving husband and a motherless daughter. My dad is still sheriff, but in a different town up the coast. Her death broke him." Eliza pulled in a shuddered breath. "And I refuse to do that to you. I thought I could have everything—I had everything under control. But it turns out that as long as I'm with you, I'm not in control. My mom tried to have both, and stupidly I have to. But it doesn't work like that—it's one or the other."

Travis took a step forward. "You're saying that you're breaking up with me so you don't destroy me?"

She gave a little nod, her eyes glistening with tears.

"I understand what you're telling me." Travis took another step forward. "But I will support you in whatever you need. I won't go running with you anymore if you feel you need to run faster. I won't surprise you with truffles. I have a salad with grilled chicken waiting for you back at the apartment. I'll do whatever it takes."

"You say that, but—"

Travis held up a hand. "Let me finish. If you think that you are sparing me by breaking up with me, then you don't understand how I feel about you. I love you, Eliza. I didn't think it would be possible for me to feel that way toward someone ever again." Her lips trembled, but he pressed on. "I love you, and maybe you'll suffer from heart problems early like your mom. Maybe you won't. We don't know. One thing I do know, though, is that if you break up with me right now—if you break up with me out of fear, then you've already caused the destruction you're trying to prevent.

"No pressure or anything, but I wake up every morning excited for the day, because I get to see you. I spend my day repairing others' homes, wondering what it would be like to work on our own home together. You make me better—you make me complete. And if you don't feel the same way toward me, then that's something I can deal with. It will suck, but I can deal with that. What I can't deal with is if you feel the same way —you want the same things—and you still choose to walk away."

The words had tumbled out so quickly, and with each word he'd drawn closer to Eliza, begging her to understand how deep his love went for her. When he finished, he was standing directly in front of her, taking her hands in his. His gaze remained on her, looking for any indication that his words had made a difference.

"My mom left me when I was six years old," she finally said, her gaze dropping to the ground, and she pulled her hands from his. "Because she loved my dad and didn't care about the repercussions. After she died, every day I would go to our corner in the library, and I would sit. I couldn't even bring myself to pull out a book and look at the pictures. I just sat, thinking of her. Wishing she was there with me. And then the only real, tangible memory I had of her was destroyed when the library succumbed to that storm only a year later." She shook her head, still refusing to meet his gaze. "I'm sorry, but...I can't do that. To you. To whatever future little girl we might have. I can't."

And then she stepped around him and ran as hard as she could.

Away.

And Travis knew he wasn't supposed to follow.

So he just sat, much like Eliza must have in the library all those years ago.

And like that little girl, he grieved for what might have been.

But there was a difference this time.

The woman Travis grieved was lost, but she wasn't gone.

In some ways that made it worse, but it also allowed for one thing Eliza hadn't had when she was little.

Hope.

## 24

Eliza had never worked so hard in her life. She ran twice her usual distance every morning and every evening. She knew the women on her volleyball team would rebel if she tried making them practice any harder, so she practiced twice as hard for them.

And when the weekend arrived and folks from the next town arrived for their game, her team crushed them.

She could admit that it had been due more her than the team as a whole. Really, she had been a one-woman show, flying from one end to the other, Bree and the others jumping out of the way as she'd go for the ball.

It wasn't how the game was supposed to be played, and she knew it. The other women were currently not talking to her, and she deserved that. But she didn't know how else to pretend her heart didn't ache every waking moment for the man she'd pushed away—for the life she'd given up.

He loved her.

After knowing each other for only two months, he loved her. Travis had said she made him a better person—he saw a future with her.

Eliza had never entertained the idea of having someone to share her life with until Travis.

And now she acted like none of those things had mattered.

And she hated herself for it.

Everything about her, in that moment and every moment since, made her feel like an awful human being.

But she didn't know what to do about it.

Eliza's life was imploding around her, and she just stood in the middle, waiting for the inevitable.

Why had God cursed her with this genetic mistake? Why wasn't she allowed to just be happy?

Now, every day was nothing but Eliza running from one thing to another, trying to forget that she was miserable and that she didn't have to be.

It was difficult to forget what she could have had when the man she loved was everywhere.

Eliza would walk the long way if she caught a glimpse of Travis, or avoid town events if she knew he'd be there.

Her insanity eventually reached a level that led to her own volleyball team handing in their resignations. They refused to attend any more games with her, so they forfeited the competition.

So now, she was more alone than she ever had been.

Had her mother gone through this? Had she tried to escape the inevitable, only to give in and allow life to happen, regardless of the consequences?

It was too late now. Eliza was too far gone.

The next two months passed like this.

September was just around the corner, and tourist season was beginning to wind down. Eliza had fewer distractions, and that wasn't good. What she needed was another visit to Patty's office. Another blood test.

When Eliza walked in, the doctor looked up from where she

sat doing paperwork behind the front desk. She cocked her head to the side and raised an eyebrow that said, *Really?*

"Please, Patty. I need this."

Patty released a long sigh and leaned back in her chair. "You've been coming in every two weeks for the past two months. You already know what it's going to say. Your numbers are coming back down, just like you knew they would. In fact, they are better than your numbers have ever been. But it's not healthy for you to be pushing yourself like this."

"But the numbers are good."

Didn't Patty see that she needed those numbers? She was going to live a long life because she took care of herself. People had told her there was nothing she could do, that she just needed to accept the fact that it was hereditary and take her medicine like a good girl.

But Eliza had beat the system. She didn't need medication. She was healthy.

"The numbers aren't everything." Patty stood and walked out to join Eliza in the waiting room. She leaned against the counter, her arms folded across her chest. "You aren't happy, Eliza. But it's more than that. You have people worried."

Eliza took a step back, not wanting to hear from another person how she needed to slow down. She had to know that her sacrifices had been the right decision—that they were worth it. That was what the numbers gave her—validation.

"I'm fine. I just need my bloodwork done, and I'll be on my way."

Patty watched Eliza long enough for it to become uncomfortable, then said, "The insurance won't pay for any more tests. In fact, they haven't covered the last five. I have. Come back in six months."

"You... You've been paying for my bloodwork?" Another thing for her to feel guilty about—another way she was hurting others. When would it stop? Eliza slumped into the nearest chair. "I'll pay you back."

Patty pushed off the counter and sat in the chair next to her. "I don't want you to pay me back. I want you to get better. And more blood tests aren't going to do it. I thought if you saw the consistent progress you were making, it might help you settle down a bit. As your doctor, I'm sorry I didn't intervene sooner."

"I can't do it anymore," Eliza managed to choke out before sobs racked her chest—all the pent-up fear and frustration and anger and guilt bursting through. Eliza was drowning, and she didn't know which way the surface was. There had been life preservers and lifeguards, but she'd pushed them all away, leaving her alone and sinking to the bottom of the ocean.

Patty stroked Eliza's hair as she cried. "I know, sweetie. I know."

When Eliza had finally cried all the tears that could be cried, Patty pulled her to her feet and gave her the longest, tightest, and most needed hug Eliza had ever had.

"Thank you," she mumbled against Patty's shoulder. She was embarrassed and exhausted, and when she pulled back, she realized she didn't have the faintest idea where to go from there. "I've burned all my bridges, Patty. I've been so horrible to everyone. They must hate me."

Patty smiled and brushed a hand against Eliza's cheek, sweeping away a stray tear. "No one hates you. They're just waiting for their Eliza to return, that's all. You might have gone a bit overboard—"

Eliza gave her a pointed look.

"Okay, a lot overboard, but this town is your family, and no one is going anywhere. Including your hardware man."

A weight settled in Eliza's stomach, and she felt sick. "He loved me. He was nothing but good to me. And then I basically gave him the middle finger and ran away. Like, I literally ran away. I haven't seen or talked to him in over two months, and that's hard to do in this town."

"It's not so hard in tourist season, and heaven knows you've kept busy."

It was true. Eliza had taken on so many jobs, she already had more money in her bank account than she had had after the entire tourist season of the previous year.

"Even so, I doubt he'll ever speak to me again. He's probably already planning where he's going to go next."

And it was all Eliza's fault.

For good reason, though, she reminded herself.

Eliza would never, ever, do to him what her mother had done to her. She couldn't allow it.

So where did that leave her?

Patty stood when the front door opened. "I wouldn't write him off yet. But you could always practice your apologies with her." She nodded toward the door, where Bree had just entered, her little son in her arms.

Bree froze, her gaze darting between Eliza and Patty. Like she knew she needed to come in for her appointment but she didn't want to.

Eliza stood and straightened her shirt. She didn't need to worry about smeared mascara, because it had been six weeks since she'd worn any makeup at all.

Tears pricked at her eyes, and the dam felt like it might burst again. Eliza hurried forward before it had the chance and wrapped her arms awkwardly around Bree and her son.

"I'm sorry. I'm so, so sorry. You just wanted to have fun, and I ruined it all. I made it about me and my issues, and you didn't deserve that. I promise, I'll never ask you to join a sports team again—just please tell me that you're still my friend."

Bree's arm reached around and held Eliza's shoulder. "Of course. That's all I ever wanted."

Eliza pulled back, angry at the tears that never seemed to run out, but also hopeful. This was one friend back, and only two hundred and twelve to go. Roughly speaking.

"Thank you." Eliza held onto Bree's free hand tightly, like she was afraid that if she let go, Bree would change her mind. But her friend merely gave her a warm smile, squeezed her hand, then pried her hand free so her little boy could have his appointment.

This felt good—right. The least insane Eliza had been in two months.

But the fear remained—it hadn't been eradicated.

The fear that said if she let her guard down, her heart issues would sneak-attack from the dark corners where they lay in wait —waiting for Eliza to lose focus.

She pulled in a deep breath and released it just as slowly.

A life with heart issues—a life on medication—it couldn't be worse than the life she was living right now.

Maybe it was worth the risk.

## 25

Travis looked at the name in his address book for a long time. He turned off his phone, then turned it back on. Did he want to call Davis? Nope. He didn't have the slightest desire to ever talk to that man again.

He wasn't a bad guy, Travis had to remind himself. The fact that Chloe had chosen him probably meant he was a better guy than even Travis was.

*You weren't good enough to hold onto Eliza.*

The thought had plagued him for two months now. Telling him he didn't measure up. Telling him he'd always be the guy women wanted to date but never marry.

Maybe that inner voice was right.

But he had seen Eliza play in her volleyball game a couple of months back. Travis knew she wouldn't have wanted him there watching, but he'd gone anyway. She had been fierce—and not in a good way.

Eliza had dominated the volleyball court, taking shots that her teammates could have easily gotten. They'd won, sure. But it hadn't been the way the game was supposed to be played.

He'd heard how the rest of the team had quit after that. They had forfeited the competition.

She wasn't the same woman he had grown to love. She was spiraling.

And Travis couldn't do anything to help her. He'd see her from a distance, and she'd turn in a different direction. He'd texted her shortly after she'd broken up with him—just once.

He'd never received a reply.

For two months, he'd felt helpless. For two months, he'd wondered what he was even doing sticking around Starlight Ridge.

Travis had contemplated telling Davis that he was done—he was moving on somewhere else. The only problem was that he'd fallen in love, not only with Eliza, but with Starlight Ridge as well. He couldn't imagine leaving Jessie and Patty and Erwin and Isaac, and everyone else. They'd become a part of his life. And he liked it. He liked going out and fixing things around town, and yeah, tourist season was insane, but he found that it was the good kind of insane. The kind that kept him guessing and never left him bored.

His lips twitched up at the corners as he realized how far he'd come since he'd arrived in town several months earlier.

When Travis had realized he didn't want to leave Starlight Ridge, the next decision came easily.

Maybe Eliza didn't want to be with him anymore...maybe it was too much pressure. Maybe he'd moved too fast.

But that didn't mean he couldn't help her.

Travis knew he wasn't the only one who was worried about Eliza—the whole town was.

Which was why he was sitting in his office, contemplating calling the one man he'd sworn he never would.

Before he could lose his nerve, he touched the call icon.

Travis put the phone on speaker, but there had been no need. It went straight to voicemail.

Of course.

When working in the middle of the Thai jungle, cell reception was not a luxury that came easily. They only had access via a satellite phone. After living that life for so long, it was troubling to him that he'd already forgotten.

He sent an email to Chloe instead. Another thing he hadn't thought he'd ever do. Simply told her that when she got the chance, could she have Davis give him a call on the satellite phone.

Travis leaned back in his chair and released a long breath.


IT TOOK two days for him to receive the call.

"Hey, everything okay?" Davis asked, his voice laced with concern.

Travis realized he could have phrased his email differently. It had been so concise, it probably sounded like an emergency. And yet it had still taken two days for Davis to call—that just showed how out of touch they'd been in the middle of nowhere.

"Yeah, things are fine. Mostly. Sorry to bother you. I just had a quick question."

And then Travis filled Davis in on what they were trying to do with the library, how they had only been able to raise half of what they'd been hoping, and he was wondering if Davis had any contractor contacts near Starlight Ridge who might be willing to offer discounted services.

"Of course. I'll send out a few emails when I get the chance and ask them to get in touch with you."

And then there were a few polite pleasantries exchanged, and that was that.

Travis's chest felt a little lighter. That hadn't been so bad.

Now to contact his wholesale suppliers.

One way or another, they were going to get this library built.

THINGS WENT a lot slower than Travis would have liked, and there was a lot of bureaucracy that he hadn't foreseen running into. A couple of Davis's contacts were interested—it looked good for them to do volunteer work in the community, and there were tax incentives. Same with his wholesale contacts. But they had to get permission from several different people, all the way up the company's hierarchy, which also included multiple rounds of signatures.

And then there were the permits. The paperwork never seemed to end. But after another month, Travis thought he finally had it all in place. And with tourist season all but dead, it was perfect timing.

As long as the town helped with labor, Starlight Ridge was going to get its library.

TRAVIS SLIPPED his phone from his pocket and touched the phone icon.

"Hey, Jessie. It's Travis. How do you get flyers made around here? We're about to have the biggest event of the season. Even bigger than the auction. And I could use your help."

Travis knew how the woman loved throwing big events, and he wasn't disappointed with her reaction.

"Ooh, really. Do tell. I don't suppose you'll need baked goods at this event, will you?"

That wasn't a bad idea. Those who didn't have the skills to build could help keep everyone fed. It would be like a good old-fashioned barn raising. Of sorts.

"We'll need all you can spare."

That was all Jessie needed to hear. "Count me in. And I can have the flyers finished within the hour."

Two weeks later. A Saturday.

Demolition day.

Barriers had been placed around the remnants of the library, and the excavator and its crew were in place.

The entire town had gathered for the event, it seemed, the excitement in the air palpable, though the children did express disappointment that they wouldn't see a wrecking ball in action.

Travis laughed and ruffled the hair on one of the complaining boys. "Sorry, kid. Too much debris. Too many safety hazards. Can't have a piece of metal shooting off in your direction, yeah?"

This didn't seem to make them feel any better, their murmured complaints continuing, albeit quieter now.

"Just talked to the site manager," Jessie said, wandering over. "Looks like they'll be starting any minute now. I know it will be a bit anticlimactic and will take all weekend to complete, but it's still exciting, isn't it?"

Travis nodded. "That it is." Peace settled within his chest, and he released a long breath. The only thing that would have made this moment better was if he could have shared it with Eliza.

Eliza.

His gaze whipped to Jessie. "Where's Eliza?"

"You told me to keep the demolition a secret."

Panic replaced the peace from moments before. Yes, he'd orchestrated the rebuilding of the library for the town. But more than that, he'd done it for Eliza. For what she'd lost. And she wasn't even going to be here to see it.

"I told you that to buy me some time. I didn't think y'all

would actually manage to keep it from her. With something this big, how is it possible that she doesn't know?"

Jessie already had her phone out by the time Travis had finished speaking, but she gave a quick shake of her head. "Phone's going straight to voicemail."

Travis turned and sprinted toward Eliza's home up the street. He made better time than he'd thought possible, all thanks to his daily runs. He'd gotten in the habit while dating Eliza, and it had felt wrong to stop. It wasn't lost on him that the day after the breakup, when he and Eliza had shown up on the beach at the same time, she had changed her schedule so their paths no longer crossed.

Travis rang Eliza's doorbell and then pounded on the door. It probably sounded like either an emergency or someone was trying to break in.

He would take either if it got her to answer the door.

Sound of the deadbolt sliding.

Travis's breath hitched.

This would be the first time he'd spoken to Eliza since the evening she'd broken up with him—the evening she'd ground his heart to dust.

A pause.

She must have seen it was him, and she was trying to decide if she should open the door.

But then she did.

And Travis didn't give her time to rethink that decision. "Good, you're already wearing shoes."

And then he grabbed her hand and pulled her from the house.

"Travis, what—"

He reached around her to pull the door shut, then hurried away from the house, Eliza in tow.

"They are going to start soon, and I'm sorry I told people not to tell you. I wanted it to be a surprise, but nothing in this town is ever a surprise. Until today, I guess. I just wanted time to get things in place. But then you didn't show up."

Eliza had been following along, allowing herself to be led, but it must have been out of shock, because she put on the brakes, snatched her hand from his, and folded her arms across her chest.

It wasn't until that moment that Travis realized she was wearing her robe, and what he had taken for sandals were more like slippers.

Oh, right. It was still early. Demolition was scheduled to begin at eight o'clock sharp.

Still, Eliza was the type to have already been up for two hours.

She took a step back, looking wary.

"Why are you acting like this...as if this is who we are now? Like you can just show up on my doorstep and whisk me away on a random adventure?"

Travis knew that was probably what it looked like. But he didn't have time to explain things again. He glanced over his shoulder toward the library. The excavator was already moving. It would rip out its first chunk of wall in just a few seconds.

"I'm not, I swear. But...look." And he gestured behind him, knowing that words would have no impact on Eliza.

Her eyes widened, like she was just noticing the crowd of people gathered further down the road. The barriers. The heavy machinery.

"The library." Her words were soft—unbelieving. "They're tearing it down."

Travis gave a small nod, then his gaze found his shoes. "And rebuilding it. Construction begins once they get all the debris cleared and the ground ready. We could really use your help."

In his panic, he'd not fully prepared for what her presence

would do to him. It tied his stomach in knots, and he felt like he was going to be sick. How could Eliza not see things from his perspective—how did she not understand what she was doing to him—what she'd done to herself?

"*My* help?"

Travis's gaze slowly rose until it met hers. "The contractors will be running the show, but anything that isn't ultra-specialized, they need our help with. That's how I was able to get the project under budget. And I can't think of anyone in town I'd rather have working by my side than you."

Eliza's breath hitched as her gaze landed just over Travis's shoulder. He turned and watched as the first piece of wall came tumbling to the ground. The crowd cheered, though there seemed to be some tears in the mix.

"Thank you." Eliza's voice was soft and genuine.

Travis turned to face her and was surprised to see that Eliza's expression was no longer guarded, seeking a way to escape. "Thank you for this. For everything."

"Anyone would have done it."

Eliza gave a slow shake of her head. "But they didn't." She pulled in a shuddered breath. "You know, I always prided myself on being the strongest in town. I could do any job that anyone gave me. It turns out I was wrong. I don't have the strength that I thought I did. The fortitude. Not like you. So, congratulations. You win."

Travis watched her, wondering how to respond to that. Because that wasn't what he was trying to do here. "It's not a competition. It never was."

"I know. But I don't know how to not turn it into one." She released a humorless laugh. "I run away from hard things. And I pretend. And I outdo everyone around me—keep myself on top. Keep everyone else at a distance. I've been doing it since the storm took out that library."

Travis could see the pain in Eliza's expression—the longing for something different, but not knowing how to allow herself to take it. He took a tentative step forward and reached a hand toward hers. When she didn't move away, he took it and clung on like his life depended on it.

"It's time for the library to have a new beginning. Don't you think you're entitled to one too?"

Eliza gave a tiny nod, and then a flicker of light passed over her expression.

Hope.

## 26

E liza walked into the hardware store and laid her work belt on the counter. Mitchell and his son had managed to botch another DIY project and called her in a panic. It had been a tough job, but she was glad she'd been the one to do it.

"Honey, I'm home," she called as she stretched her arms above her head and twisted side to side. A couple pops in her back. She sighed in relief and lowered her arms.

Travis poked his head out of the office and smiled. "How'd it go?"

"Oh, about the only way it can when you call Eliza Meyer to fix three holes in your wall where there had previously only been one. So, it went beautifully, of course. I still don't know how they managed to triple the damage while attempting the repair, though."

Eliza liked to complain, but really, she wouldn't have it any other way. Ever since she'd watched their library's demolition, she knew she wanted more from life than passing out flyers and watching people's cats. She wanted to be a part of helping her town grow and thrive. She wanted to build.

It had been a tough interview. Travis had asked some hard

questions, but in the end, after a few calls to some carefully selected references, he'd offered Eliza a job at the hardware store. Now they were able to do twice the business he'd been doing before.

"Mitchell has skills that elude even the best of us," Travis said. "Which is why business is doing so well. Speaking of, I just talked to Davis."

Eliza wandered over to the bathroom to clean up. "Yeah?"

It always made Eliza nervous when a sentence started with *I just talked to Davis.*

She always worried that he'd decide Thailand wasn't for him and he'd return—take back his store. And where would that leave Eliza and Travis?

Together. And whatever happened, they'd figure it out.

"He's really liking it in Thailand."

Travis was stalling.

"That's nice. He deserves happiness."

She held her breath as she scrubbed the dirt from under her nails, then cast an anxious look over her shoulder. She hoped this wasn't bad news.

Travis was watching her through the open doorway, grinning. He was purposely trying to make her nervous.

Eliza spun around and flicked water on him. "You going to tell me what's going on or am I going to have to drag it out of you?"

Curses. She'd given him the reaction he was looking for. He always knew just which buttons to push.

"Seems like Davis is looking to sell."

Eliza released a small squeal. That was better news than she could have hoped for. Travis deserved this—a place of his own.

"I'm so happy for you." Eliza leaped forward and planted a big kiss on Travis's lips. She pulled away but kept her hands on either side of his face. "I'm assuming you're going to buy it, yes?"

Travis raised a shoulder, like he didn't care either way. "Thinking about it. Except I was thinking more along the lines that *we* could buy it." And then he grinned, like this was the best news of all.

Eliza's hands dropped to her sides, and she took a step back. Panic. This was a big commitment that Travis was suggesting. What if something went south in their relationship? That would be all kinds of bad.

Not to mention, there was one surprise she had of her own that she hadn't yet shared.

Travis's excitement faltered. "Only if you want to, of course. I would never force you into anything. It's just... I was hoping..."

Seeming to make up his mind, Travis dropped to one knee.

Oh, gosh. Was this happening? Was the man of Eliza's dreams about to propose? On the dirty floor of a hardware store bathroom?

"Eliza Meyer, will you do me the honor of—" His words broke off, and he seemed to take in the less-than-ideal surroundings for the first time. "Nope. Not going to do it this way."

And then the man had the audacity to get up, walk across the hall to his office, and proceed to do inventory.

And Eliza was left staring.

"I'm sorry? You're just going to go back to work after—" Words failed her.

Travis glanced back, his lips twitching up at the corners.

"Oh. You wanted to do this now?" He released a dramatic sigh. "Very well, then."

He grabbed Eliza by the hand, and before she could protest, he pulled her through the back entrance of the store. There, on a path hidden among the palm trees and foliage, were two large palm leaves that had been arranged in the shape of a heart. Candles were lit along the heart's edges, and in the middle sat three small boxes. Ring boxes.

Relief coursed through her, and love for the unpredictably sweet and perfect Travis Matkin. The one she'd sworn she'd never fall for.

Except, why were there three boxes? Was this the kind of game where only one box held the ring, and if she chose incorrectly, she lost?

Eliza threw a questioning glance at Travis.

He merely smiled and said, "Choose one."

She pointed to the one in the middle, but Travis picked up the box on the left instead and brought it to her. Her lips quirked up into a smile, and she lifted the lid.

Inside was a small pair of wooden running shoes with a hole in the top and a chain running through it, perfectly complementing the wooden barbell he'd made for her when she'd been sick with the flu.

"It's beautiful," she said, giving him a kiss.

Travis pulled her in tight. "I would never ask you to stop running, Eliza. But I am asking that you allow me to run with you on whatever crazy adventures this life brings us." He nodded to the boxes. "Choose another."

She chose the middle box.

And once again, Travis ignored her choice, instead picking up the box on the right and handing it to her.

When she opened it, she discovered another wooden pendant. This one was a diploma. Her breath caught. "You know?"

Travis smiled. "I also would never ask you to give up your dreams for me. I did hear that you have been accepted into the doctor of physical therapy program. And you should absolutely go for it. I only ask you to allow me to be your number one cheerleader."

Tears pricked at her eyes, and she smiled. Only one box left.

Eliza pointed to the same one she'd been pointing to all along.

But Travis didn't pick it up this time either. Instead, he pulled a fourth box from his pocket and kneeled in front of Eliza.

"I know this life hasn't been fair to you," he said. "And you have a lot of reasons to say no. But I believe you have even more reasons to say yes." Travis pulled a folded piece of paper from his pocket and handed it to her.

Eliza opened it and stifled a laugh.

It was a resume. For Travis.

"Excellent health-conscious cook," she read. "Can fix things, but only what Eliza doesn't want to do herself. Loves children and dogs, not necessarily in that order..."

Eliza had to stop because the tears that had merely pricked at her eyes moments before were now threatening to turn into a flash flood.

She glanced away from the paper to Travis and saw that he'd opened the box, and a beautiful ring sat inside.

"Will you—"

Eliza tackled him to the ground and said, "Yes. Of course. Yes." She kissed him, her lips exploring his, frantic. "And we can buy the hardware store together, and I'll open up my own physical therapy center. As far as living quarters, though, I think we should live in my house. I mean, my parents left it to me, and it has a lot more space than the apartment. And despite my earlier reservations, I'd love kids. And dogs. But not the yappy kinds. That goes for both the kids and the dogs. And—"

Her insane rambling was stopped by Travis moving in for another kiss.

"I only want you to marry me if you feel good about this," he said when he pulled back. "I don't want you worried about what might or might not happen. If your cholesterol goes weird next week or something—I don't want my proposal to be the source of your stress. Besides, you sure you can handle all of this?" He used a hand to gesture to the entire length of his body.

Eliza grinned. "Dude. I could bench press you. And I know there will be some momentary freak-outs in my future. But I also know that you'll help me come back from them. You've helped me to rediscover the life that I want to live—the one I'm meant to live. And I'm madly in love with everything about you. How could I say no to something like that?"

Travis jumped up and then helped Eliza to her feet.

"I'm curious, though," she said as he blew out the candles. "What was in the box in the middle?"

He gave her a sheepish smile, straightened, and handed it to her. "A chocolate truffle. But..." Pink tinged his cheeks as she opened it. The box was empty. "I kind of ate it."

She burst into laughter. "Then why put it with the others?"

"It looked weird without it."

And that was the moment that confirmed that Eliza wanted to spend the rest of her life with Travis Matkin. And even longer, if that was allowed.

# EPILOGUE

E rwin pounded in another nail, grateful for the chance to be a part of the rebuilding of the library. He wasn't exactly the first guy people called when they needed help with manual labor, and he didn't often have the opportunity. That wasn't to say he *couldn't* do it. Erwin had some hidden talents of his own. He took pride in always fixing what he could and rarely needed to call Davis, or now Travis.

Despite the late-September breeze, sweat beaded along his brow, and he swiped at it with the back of his hand.

Jessie was walking among the volunteers with cups of lemonade and trays of baked goods should he need a rest. But no one else had taken a rest yet, and neither would he.

If only Erwin's back would stop aching, complaining that he'd been crouched in that one position too long. He hated to admit it, but it seemed somewhere along the way, he'd gotten old. Of course, fifty-nine wasn't all that old in the scheme of things, was it? He still had plenty of life ahead of him.

But compared to the young guys—men like Travis and Isaac and even Caleb—he didn't move as fast as he used to.

As if sensing that Erwin needed a break that he so stubbornly refused to take, Jessie wandered over, lemonade in one hand, a bottle of water in the other.

"You're going to kill yourself trying to keep up with these guys," she said, offering him the water. After all those years, she still remembered his dislike of anything lemon.

Erwin grunted and took the bottle. "I can keep up with the best of them. Don't you forget that I stood on a ladder outside your second-story windows for two hours while fixing those shutters of yours."

Jessie's lips twitched up into a smile. "That you did. And then Davis had to return and fix them again two years later."

"That was two years I didn't have to listen to them slamming against the side of your house at all hours of the night." He took a pull from his water bottle. Nothing had ever tasted so good.

A pause.

"I did appreciate it, you know." Jessie's voice was surprisingly soft. "It had been a rough summer, with me closing up my bakery. Even though I'd always planned on retiring early, I underestimated how sad it would make me. How lost I would feel. It's funny... You wouldn't think that picking up the phone to call Davis or taking a stroll over to the hardware store would be that difficult. But I couldn't bring myself to do it—or much of anything else, for that matter. Even though, yes, those shutters were annoying as hell and kept me up all night. You really did save my sanity that summer."

Erwin's gaze rose just enough to see the sincerity behind her eyes. "For the record, I think you did right, closing up shop. You seem happier now, working and baking on your own terms. Not having to cater to the tourists."

Jessie held out a hand, and it took a moment for Erwin to realize she was expecting him to give her his empty water bottle —he hadn't even realized he'd drained it.

She tucked it into a bag that hung from her shoulder and

turned away, but then paused. "It's only too bad that I had to go it alone. These past few decades—it would have been a hell of an adventure."

And then she walked away, her steps starting out slow, but by the time she'd reached the refreshment table, she was practically skipping, a smile on her face as she reached forward to help a small boy with a brownie he couldn't quite manage to grab on his own.

A wave of guilt and regret washed over Erwin. That hadn't been Jessie's intention, he knew. She never allowed herself to stay down long—never allowed herself to be sad. She was the epitome of pulling herself up by her bootstraps.

But Jessie shouldn't have had to pull herself up. She should have been able to have the adventure she'd always dreamed of. With someone by her side, sharing the load. Someone that loved her more than their own ambitions.

And it was Erwin's fault she hadn't found that.

Because she'd been stuck with him as a fiancé all those years ago, when they were young and had all those ideas of how life was going to go.

And it was him who had ruined it all.

And it was him who desperately wished he could rewind time and have a chance to do it all over again.

Because if given the chance, he'd never have let Jessie go.


*The End*

# ALSO BY KAT BELLEMORE

# ABOUT THE AUTHOR

Kat Bellemore is the author of the Borrowing Amor small town romance series. Deciding to have New Mexico as the setting for the series was an easy choice, considering its amazing sunsets, blue skies and tasty green chile. That, and she currently lives there with her husband and two cute kids. They hope to one day add a dog to the family, but for now, the native animals of the desert will have to do. Though, Kat wouldn't mind ridding the world of scorpions and centipedes. They're just mean.

You can visit Kat at www.kat-bellemore.com.

Made in the USA
Middletown, DE
01 April 2022

63442631R00123